Upheaval

By

Sherie L. Howard

For my son Michael

I love you always

CHAPTER ONE

ALASKA

Swarms of tiny tremors shook the ground eighty miles west of

Anchorage. During the last six weeks, there had been fifty-eight

minor earthquakes around the base of Mount Spurr, each one had

gone unnoticed by most people in the area, except by Paul Wabel,

the head volcanologist and seismologist at the National Earthquake

Information Center (NEIC) in Alaska, who had taken precautions for

the sake of public safety, by sending his team on an expedition to

Crater Peak, a vent on the south side of Spurr, one that had erupted twenty-seven years earlier, taking the life of Paul's best friend, Eddie Locklear.

"I need to know what type of gases are being released." He addressed his team, consisting of young, intelligent, and adventurous types from the University of Anchorage, students who were in the process of earning a Master's Degree in Geological Science, and those who would someday be battling for his job, the volcanologist and seismologist in charge of the Ring of Fire. "Chris, I also want to know the amount of gases being released." He looked directly at the team leader. "Check movement."

"Absolutely." Chris' answers were always sharp, without delay. He would have checked for movement regardless. He knew better than to come back minus a full report.

Paul nodded. He was known coast to coast for his thorough reports and had spent over twenty years collecting samples from active volcanoes. Spurr was one of them, an appropriately named giant who was capable of impulsive and unplanned actions. Paul had warned his friend Eddie not to walk too close to the rim of the crater.

That was in 1992, after Paul and Eddie had each completed a Bachelor's Degree in Geological Science at The University of Anchorage, an accomplishment that they decided to celebrate by taking a week-long hiking trip, one that would take them up and around Spurr's Crater Peak, a trip that was supposed to unwind them, before diving into a more advanced program – a Master's Degree in Volcanology and Geological Hazards.

She's upset today Eddie. Stay clear of the rim. They were words that fell on deaf ears. Eddie had turned twenty-six, two days earlier, but often acted like a teenager. *Careless* and *negligent* in Paul's opinion, adjectives that Paul Wabel wouldn't tolerate describing his team. He had lost enough people in his life, including his own father who lost his life in a boating accident when Paul was a baby.

"I don't want any heroics." He looked into the eyes of his young team members, one at a time, making sure each one understood the risks. Paul had recently turned fifty-two years old, and spent most of his time in the laboratory or in his office, studying volcanic behavior, predicting eruptions, and analyzing printouts, all in an effort to warn people who resided anywhere near the Ring of Fire of any possible eruption. "I have a zero-tolerance for risk-takers." He stated before his team left. "Anyone who fucks up and exhibits any gung-ho bullshit will be dismissed from my class." He was referring to the class he taught on Tuesday nights at The University of Anchorage, titled *Lava and Life*.

"Yes, Mr. Wabel." Once again, it was the voice of the team leader, Chris, a twenty-three-year-old, who planned on beating out all of his teammates for Wabel's job someday. "I will make sure the EDM and the COSPEC instruments are placed in a safe location, as well as the three infrared cameras." Chris was referring to the instruments that measured ground deformation and volcanic gases.

"I want the VLF set up too." Paul Wabel directed his comment to Chris. Thinking about his friend Eddie Locklear, Paul wanted to see if the underground lava movement was increasing. Something Eddie always believed would trigger a major earthquake.

"Will do sir." Chris turned, then ordered his teammates toward the exit. They were all expert climbers and paid attention to detail when prepping for a climb. It was a dangerous hike, one that would retire proper gear and planning, but Paul needed the information, and he wanted to make sure the recent activity at Mount Spurr was nothing to worry about, and that public safety wasn't being threatened. He took a lot of pride in his work. If there were two words that described Paul Wabel, they would be *scientific* and *cautious*. Endless hours were spent recording and studying activity from the volcanoes within the Pacific Ring of Fire, all 452 of them, and having the position of head volcanologist and seismologist in an area known for the world's most powerful eruptions, was a dream career, and one he had often imagined having since he was a young boy, a time that was filled with stories about the magic powers contained in mountains and volcanoes.

Although fairytales had never interested Paul, he often stared out his office window, looking directly across Cook Inlet at a mountain his mother and others in Anchorage referred to as Sleeping Lady. It wasn't a volcano, but was near several, and was hard to overlook as he stared across the water at Mount Spurr, the one that seemed to keep watch over Sleeping Lady, and the one that had taken Eddie's life.

He knew the shape of Sleeping Lady mountain was purely coincidental, nothing more; even though he remembered most of his childhood friends swearing it was a real lady, asleep on her side, the back of her head facing Cook Inlet with long wavy hair that glistened in the sunlight, a shapely rounded shoulder reaching toward the sky, and a tiny waist that swooped inward at the middle, which led into what his best friend Eddie, in their teenage years, and even into college, called a shapely ass – one that extended into long fuck me legs.

When Paul turned forty-five, he retired his climbing gear, but even confined to 'his office, he still felt a connection to the volcanoes that surrounded Sleeping Lady. He considered them his immediate family, and he believed his extended family stretched 25,000 miles into the Pacific Ocean, as far south as Australia on the western side of the Ring of Fire, and down the west coast of North America and South America, on the eastern side of the ring.

Scientists counted on his data and used his records to determine patterns and make predictions about future activity in the Ring of Fire, and even in other areas around the globe. Paul routinely received consultation calls seeking his opinion about earthquakes and their possible correlation to volcanic activity. He had plenty of data, especially over the last couple of days, since his team had safely returned, and since there had been another increase in tremors around Mount Spurr, the volcano known by the indigenous people in the area as K'idazq'eni. Paul Wabel knew the native name meant *burning inside*, but he didn't take the name seriously, and preferred to stick to the scientific facts, which had resulted in numerous entries in his ledger.

After carefully examining the information he had collected from the EDM, COSPEC and VLF instruments, he accessed The World Disaster Data Bank on his computer to record his findings: **Volcanic tremors were, and continue to be, triggered by glacial activity and will not cause an eruption.** *No worries.* He thought. For a brief moment he studied the VLF report – *increased lava.* He knew the information would download into the system, something his dead friend would have insisted be shared with the public. Paul would document the information, even though he knew Eddie was wrong. *Increased lava movement will not cause a volcano to erupt.*

Then he finished his private thought, one he had repeated to himself throughout grad school. *Volcanic activity, from glaciers or lava movement, will not trigger an earthquake.* It was scientific fact. Pure and simple.

At 3:30 p.m. on the twenty-first of August, Paul Wabel's scientific facts fell under scrutiny and were being questioned coast to coast, and even around the globe. His eyes studied the wave amplitude on the report he was currently holding, one he had reached for as soon as he heard it printing, and as soon as he regained his footing in his office. The Aleutian Islands had rocked between the Bering Sea and North Pacific Ocean, shaking Anchorage and the surrounding areas for hundreds of miles. Roadways buckled and cell towers toppled. It was bad timing to say the least. The Pacific Northwest Coast's major power grid was caught with its pants down, while being updated and serviced when the 7.2 quake hit. Other centers around the United States and government officials who had clearance were privy to the recently documented volcanic activity, something they had made sure to consult before making the decision to refurbish part of the Western Interconnection.

It was the sound of the printer, a second time, just a few minutes after the first report, that sent a cold chill through Paul's body. A second quake had occurred near another volcano within the Ring of Fire. Paul studied the second sheet of ink drawn lines. This time the epicenter hugged the coast of Ecuador, where the current time was 6:36 p.m., three hours later than it currently was in Anchorage. Paul closed his eyes, imagining the late evening commute, a time when families drove home to be with loved ones after a long day at work, a time when public transportation was at its peak, a time when middle school children played near the coastline, a time when mothers were picking up their babies from daycare, and a time when busy street markets were making their final sales.

Surely it wasn't coincidental. Surely it was the result of volcanic activity. Those were thoughts in the mind of Sam Whittaker as he dialed Paul Wabel, using the satellite phone system within the Seattle mayor's office.

"You can tell the mayor it is not a theory." Paul almost screamed into the phone, his intolerance for having to answer to the mayor's assistant was showing. "It is scientific fact." He sternly informed the voice on the other end of the phone, the one calling from Seattle, and the one that wanted to blame Paul for not giving the West Coast, specifically Washington State, the closest U.S. neighbor, a heads-up.

"We know about the recent tremors Paul." He said with a smirk. "Even near Ecuador." Both statements were supposed to remind Paul that the mayor has access to the information entered into the World Disaster Data Bank. "You shouldn't tell the world that increased volcanic activity won't cause an earthquake Paul. We moved forward on a major refurbishment based on your opinion; now, our entire coastal electrical grid has taken a shit."

"The increased volcanic tremors and movement underneath and inside of Spurr had nothing to do with the quake off the coast of Anchorage," Paul stated bluntly. "And, I guess you're referring to the volcano Guagua Pichincha, near Ecuador, which, if you would have bothered reading the data, you would know that Pichincha hasn't had any recent tremors." Then, without giving Sam Whittaker a moment more, Paul ended the call.

Over two hours passed before Paul answered his satellite phone again. This time he imagined it was about the tsunami that had hit the coast of Oregon within the last fifteen minutes. He took a deep breath, before letting a private thought fill his mind. *Hopefully, it's not another bureaucratic pussy.*

"Do you know that the twenty-first day of August in Clatsop county is evening registration for the public-school system?" It was the assistant superintendent of Clatsop county on the coast of Oregon, the same one that had helped rush parents and children into the gymnasium, and the same one that within minutes had climbed bleachers with scared kindergartners, in an effort to avoid the wall of incoming water, a deep pool that quickly covered the newly waxed basketball court flooring, drowning a ten-foot painted sandpiper on the gymnasium floor near center court.

"Sir, I am aware that today is the twenty-first of August." He paused, taking a moment to file his emotions. "I hope there were no injuries to any of your students or families." Then back to business. "I can assure you that my findings showed no concern for a possible earthquake off the coast of Alaska." Then his final address. "And,

Mount Spurr is definitely not to blame for the tsunami waves that rushed down the coast and slammed into Oregon."

Paul Wabel ended the call the same way he had ended the last one – abruptly. He knew his meticulous records would be scrutinized and questioned; after all, a 7.2 quake had shaken the ground around Anchorage and several hundred miles in each direction. It had sent adults scrambling to safety under the hazy 3:30 p.m. sky, while small children seemed to be more concerned about the fate of Mount Susitna, the formal name for the mountain summit whose silhouette looked like a sleeping lady, and one that many indigenous grandmothers and grandfathers had told endless bedtime stories about, each modified to their own families' beliefs. Paul Wabel remembered his own mother telling him stories about the summit when he was a small boy, and he remembered how she would start each story with a description of the mountain's silhouette.

Paulie, she is a sleeping lady. He often caught himself remembering his mother, as he stared out at the mountain summit, one that clearly looked like a woman asleep on her side. *Sleeping*

Lady lies on the other side of Cook Inlet and watches over you. Paulie, you will always be safe, unless she crumbles to her death, then you must run for safety. Paul was too scientific to believe in such nonsense. He knew that the silhouette of Mount Susitna was made up of rock and dirt. It was only a summit.

All the shaking in the world won't wake her. Realistic thoughts only; his mind was too scientific to believe in childhood fantasies.

#

Fifty-eight-year-old Enola May Starks, believed in childhood stories, more so as an adult, than she ever had as a child. Her childhood hadn't allowed her the luxury of believing in magic; her childhood had been about fighting for basic survival. Now, as an adult, she was open to a world full of enchantment and possibilities; every day was a new beginning.

It was that magical zest for life that inspired her to travel the Dalton Highway in Alaska, America's loneliest road, and probably one of the most dangerous. She had filled her car with two bins of food – Cup-a-Soup, canned ravioli, packaged tuna – and an overabundance of bottled water which she routinely restocked. She also loaded up on plenty of dog food, purchased an eight-inch futon mattress, packed three blankets, tossed in a thermal sleeping bag for extra warmth, and made sure the co-pilot seat was reserved for Miles, her four-legged companion that would accompany her.

After driving over 4000 miles, most of those through Canada's British Columbia and Yukon, and hundreds of those on every available roadway in south and interior Alaska, she finally began her journey on the Dalton. It was the sixteenth of August, when Enola first made an appearance on the dirt road that stretched north from Livengood, Alaska. The first fifty miles she dodged big potholes, and let her new tires fight for traction on the road's muddy surface. It had rained for three days prior, supplying enough mud to paint her Jeep a chalky brown.

Driving until the sky filled with blue and the last sprinkle fell, she pulled over as the sun started its slow descent in the western sky. The absence of rain was short-lived, as it reappeared, this time making designs in the mud canvas that covered her Jeep. Enola watched the rain wiggle down her rear hatch, one that would stay closed for the entire trip. Its ability to open and shut had been taken away by the mounted spare, a second to the first that was hidden inside the Jeep's spare tire well.

I'll never need two spares. Enola thought but then decided to take the advice of people who had made the trip before her – complete strangers, whose blogs she had read on the internet. *Two spare tires, just in case.* She finally gave in.

It was that type of preparation and persistence that had gotten her to the Arctic Ocean Shuttle in Deadhorse, eight hundred and fifty miles away from the earthquake that was shaking Anchorage. The only thing shaking near Enola, was a tan and white Jack Russell mix, as his paws fought for placement on the Arctic Ocean Shuttle's bouncy ride. Enola was aware that in eight more miles, she would be as far north as she'd ever go in her life. On the other hand, she was completely unaware that the world was breaking apart southwest of her. She was clueless.

Living the nomadic lifestyle had become the very essence of Enola, something that isolated her from mainstream society. She felt most comfortable when she was living as a wanderer, away from television, and as close to nature as possible. Off-grid for Enola made her feel normal.

This trip, she traveled roads that weren't accessible with a camper, unlike her last big adventure, the one where she had towed a thirteen-foot camper around the perimeter of the lower forty-eight states, first to visit Allie and Reese who were camping in California, then to see Dixie and Ryan who lived in North Carolina, and finally to Massachusetts so she could cross state forty-eight off her bucket list. Somewhere on the returning trip, probably on a long stretch of interstate, Enola convinced herself that buying a small house would make her appear more established, and would place her in the role of an archetypal divorced woman; Enola contradicted that view, a short time after arriving back in Spokane, she allowed her plan to settle down and develop some sort of permanency to dissolve into nothing. She yearned for more open road; this time with extra challenges. Alaska was more than another road trip; it was a dare. *You shouldn't do the Dalton alone.* She had heard that opinion many times over. *It's too dangerous.* Those words were fuel to Enola.

She balanced herself on one foot while untying her right sneaker with her left hand. Miles watched her as she pulled it off and tossed it onto the rocky coastline. After slipping off her sock, she regained her balance with both feet, before taking two large steps to the chilly water's edge. *Okay.* She thought. *Here it goes.* She placed her right foot in the Arctic Ocean, allowing the next wave to wash over the top of a small tattoo, a word that she and her daughter had shared with each other since Allie's early childhood, one that meant *I love you* in Cherokee Indian. *Gvgeyui.* Enola thought of Allie as she silently mouthed the word. *Guh-gay-you-ee.*

"Freezing." She reported the sensation to Miles, this time out loud, but left her foot there long enough to let her skin turn bright red. "You're next." She pulled back, redressing her wet foot in her sock and sneaker, before urging Miles to step in. "I did half of mine; you do half of yours." She gave him instructions, which apparently he understood, because he stepped up to the water's edge and slowly buried both front paws in the cold Arctic Ocean. His eyes were focused ten to twelve feet in front of him. "It's a spotted seal," Enola announced. "He's curious about you."

Time and space seemed endless at the moment, as Enola and Miles stared out at the less frequented body of water. The color of its ripple-coated surface matched its temperature – both a dark gray metal.

CHAPTER TWO

NINE MONTHS EARLIER

Small rocks crunched beneath my Jeep's tires, as it gingerly pulled the 1963 Happy Day's trailer, a purchase off craigslist, a fifty-five-year-old vintage camper, a couple of years younger than me. Like the camper, I was camouflaged from the rest of the world. Its leafy green paint job had been premediated by the previous owner, in an attempt to hide it from unsuspecting deer and elk on father-son weekends. My outer surface had been inaugurated by childhood abuse, shitty male companions, estranged family members, and was hardened like the crunchy lot in Los Banos, California. The rotation of each tire ground bits of rock and desert clay as it settled, something I was not; I lived like death was around the corner – passionately, effervescently, and rootless.

The cold November air in Los Banos stung my face like hurtful childhood words. *Don't label yourself with names that represent your wounds*. I reminded myself, as I ran my hand along the shape of Miles' tail, crooked since birth according to the animal shelter in Spokane, something I suspected wasn't true. Its twisted shape inched toward me. *Crook*. I recalled his name, the one I had replaced with a more appropriate one, just ten days earlier, after I stood at the Spokane Animal Shelter, where he looked at me through animal prison bars, and where without sound his face said it all. I recognized the look. *Broken. Damaged. Betrayed. Empty*. I knew immediately we had a connection, but it wasn't because of those labels, it was because of the one I could see deep inside his uniquely colored butterscotch eyes, a characteristic that I knew we both possessed – *strength*.

One hundred and seventy-five-dollars later he was mine. He strutted out of the Spokane Humane Society with confidence. We both did. *Strong. Alive. New.* And my Jack Russell co-pilot, who I promptly named *Miles*, had a name that represented my therapy – being behind the wheel of a vehicle – a machine that maneuvered rough terrain, exaggerated dips, unexpected potholes, wrong-way turns, dangerous conditions, and unplanned detours; it replicated the life I had mastered living.

I searched the dark in the large gravel lot before opening my Jeep's door to the corral of broken-down RVs, semi-truck drivers that had reached their maximum driving quota, cars that served as makeshift housing for single moms, drug addicts, cheating husbands, and young men down on their luck, most hiding from a world that they felt worked against them.

Life doesn't give you what you deserve. You have to learn how to use what you have. I reminded myself, as I clipped a leash to Miles' collar, before exiting my Jeep Cherokee, and making my way in the shadows to my camper that had been in tow, and that now blended into the night sky. I placed a silver key in the deadbolt, turned it right, until I heard the cylinder make a hard turn. *Click.* The sound registered in my mind as a voice approached me in the darkness. I recognized its intensity – warm, confident, compassionate, and cautious. It was Allie, my twenty-three-year-old daughter.

"Hey Mom." Allie addressed me, after loading her life into her own camper, and after making her way toward me.

"Hey Allie." I chirped back in the darkness, as I studied her slim form, her white camper serving as a backdrop to her silhouette.

I went in for a hug as she got close in the murky November air. Allie smelled alive, reminding me of my younger self, hair that fought for direction, a spirit that yearned to roam free, and a heart that rarely allowed people to enter. Her current exceptions were Reese, her twenty-six-year-old fiancé; Shiloh, a black lab she had rescued from the desert; Zeus, Shiloh's common-law husband; and Yoda, proof of their union and a recent surrender from the forever home that had originally pleaded to have him as a puppy, a forfeit which Allie gladly accepted back. Her heart had no limit for dogs, or cats for that matter, and had lately welcomed another addition –

Serenity, a tuxedo cat, discarded like trash in one of those secret gravel lots only known by people trying to survive.

"Make sure you lock your door Mom," Allie announced, her face fighting the end of November cold, as it nudged against my face.

"I promise," I replied. "You sleep safely too." I felt her jaw tremble from the cold.

"I love you Mom." I liked the way her face shined in the cloudy moonlight, full of spirit, and full of promise. Spending Thanksgiving and Christmas with Allie and Reese, was something I wanted, something I needed, before venturing to the east coast to see Dixie and Ryan in North Carolina, before traveling up to Massachusetts (state number forty-eight on my bucket list), and before making my way back to Spokane. "Maybe it will warm up when we visit the coast tomorrow," Allie added.

"I hope so." I wanted warmth. "Goodnight Allie." And then, "I love you." I watched her walk away, into the pitch-black night, to her life, to three dogs, to one cat, and to a twenty-six-year-old man that I hoped would guard her with his life. I clicked my deadbolt to the lock position, felt my way to the far corner of my camper, where my memory foam mattress waited for me, on a wooden platform, a stage for Miles, who was biding his time, until he found his place under several blankets. He snuggled by my side, with his crooked tail resting in the dark, his head barely visible. I could make out his puppy-dog eyes using the light from my cell phone. A color resembling brown sugar swirled around his pupils, reminding me of Bobby, a man I had met a few years back in Detroit.

Visiting Detroit, my birthplace, was something I did right after retiring. After my last year as a high school English teacher had ended, I drove from Pasco County, Florida to Jacksonville, where I caught a plane to Detroit. It was a place I had avoided visiting, since my parents decided to uproot my six-year-old self and my two-year-old sister, taking us to the mountains of North Carolina, where my father found it easier to be abusive, away from his religious friends and the small church where he had spent time conducting Sunday sermons. *Baptists have a lot of secrets.* I reminded myself, based on my own experiences.

Dacey Fears was a man who traded his Bible for a leather belt and wooden baseball bat. You can imagine my internal relief when I found out he wasn't my biological father, a secret that unraveled after I turned eighteen. My mother, Melantha Fears, wasn't happy when her life, the one made up of so many dark memories, came crashing down around her, a past full of events that most people could never survive, and a lifetime of pain that tormented her until she took her own life. I didn't find out that she had arranged the death of my biological father, Grover Starks, before executing her own, until I was well into my adult years. A part of me will always believe it was one last intentional passive-aggressive act toward me – the baby she always hated – and the one that she would make sure never got the chance to truly know her father. My time on earth with Grover Starks only lasted a few months, long enough for me to memorize his deep sea-blue eyes, ones that matched mine when I stood in the sunlight.

Now, I was looking at Miles' eyes with the light of my cell phone – a creamy butterscotch – like Bobby Harb's eyes – the ones I last saw during my 2016 summer visit to Detroit. Normally, I trusted no one, but that July I followed my gut instincts, after finding myself in an awkward situation – down Michigan Avenue, in a rough area, that Uber drivers avoided, after eating breakfast in a diner that I had walked to from my last Uber lift.

He's a regular. I convinced myself, after watching him leave a ten-dollar bill, for his breakfast – two scrambled eggs with bacon and home fries accompanied by a side of wheat toast – and after watching him extend a friendly wave to the husband and wife team behind the counter at Mike's Ham Place. They waved back like they had known him forever. That's when I let my guard down and accepted the offer that he had extended ten minutes earlier, after he had overheard my phone conversation with an Uber driver, one who refused to pick me up in that part of town.

"If the offer is still available, I would appreciate a lift to a motel near the Amtrak station." It was an announcement I made without moving from my seat, one that could be heard down the breakfast counter. *Witnesses.* I told myself.

"I don't mind at all." His voice matched his build. Strong and powerful.

"Thanks." I didn't say anything else before gathering my belongings and leaving a ten-dollar bill at my table to cover my breakfast and a tip, a replica of his, minus the scrambled eggs, and replacing them with two over-easy. I waved to the owners who seemed to watch the makings of a relationship play out in front of them.

It was true, that under other circumstances I could have easily fallen for Bobby Harb. He felt comfortable, and what would normally be an awkward silence between two strangers or an overabundance of nervous chitchat, turned out to be a free-flowing dialogue between old friends. He did not put on airs or force small talk into the tiny moments of soothing silence. Instead, our minds seemed to connect, as I imagined our bodies would too, both moving and reacting in a deep intensity.

"Do you think people choose their destiny?" He asked. His eyes wandered to the left-hand side of the road, where a woman pushed a shopping cart full of wadded clothing, tattered blankets, aged cookware, and bits and pieces that represented her life.

"I think people get tired of fighting," I answered. My mind pictured the woman living paycheck to paycheck, a societal trap that often ends in disaster, and one I imagined she found it easier to walk away from. "Sometimes people do whatever feels less stressful."

"Everyone is capable of change." He stated, then gave me room to comment.

"Definitely." I followed up. "People always have choices." Apparently, he liked my last declarative statement, as I watched him look in my direction and smile.

He looked at me more than he looked at the road, as he talked about Detroit's ups and downs. His lips seemed to match my heartbeat. Fast. I didn't take my eyes off of them, until I felt his hand brush mine, after realizing we were parked in front of The Viking Motel in Detroit, and after he handed me his cell phone number on a napkin, one he had taken from Mike's Ham Place.

"Call me if you need anything while you're in Detroit." He said.

"I will," I answered politely, but my mind was focused on the caramel-colored hand that had found a resting spot on his driver's window ledge. *Wedding band.* I wondered if my look of

disappointment showed. I knew he was good at reading me. I often

think Bobby Harb read me better than most people that I had known

for years. He knew I'd call. It was two days later. That was my best

attempt to show some restraint.

"I don't want to inconvenience you, Bobby." I liked the way

his name rolled off the tip of my tongue. "But, if you have any time

before I leave tomorrow, I'd like to see 8-Mile Road.

"You can't find an Uber driver for that area either, can you?"

He laughed, his way of telling me he was kidding.

"I didn't try," I answered, without laughing, my way of

telling him that I wanted to be with him.

It was a Friday evening drive, down one of the most

dangerous neighborhoods in America. There is a thick dividing line

between poor and wealthy, and 8-Mile didn't know wealthy. It only

knew devastation. I could tell that Bobby didn't judge the people we

passed, nor did he turn a blind eye toward the world of drugs and

crime. Something about Bobby was special. I saw it in the diner, and

I saw it as he chauffeured me down 8-Mile. He looked inside of people.

The goodbye between us at the end of the day ended without action, just a simple touch of hands, mine absent of a wedding band, and his, the one sporting a solid gold band, stayed intact, respecting the God he had faith in.

It was the same God he had worshipped at a mosque a few weeks later in Detroit – Bobby Harb's last day alive – one that I inadvertently learned about as I read the major headline stories in *USA Today* following my trip. The small black and white photo didn't do him justice, but I knew it was him after my imagination colored butterscotch into his eyes and painted his skin a light caramel. I read the italicized print underneath his photo: *Bobby Harb, 43, gunned down by his brother after exiting a Detroit mosque.*

CHAPTER THREE

OREGON

Twenty-four hundred watts of power raged through the siren in

Seaside, at precisely six-fifty p.m. At first people paid no heed to the

wailing siren, assuming it was only a test tone, a mandatory routine,

but then realized it wasn't the normal test day for the month. Not on

a Wednesday. The shrieking tone escalated to a higher pitch within

seconds, grabbing Allie's attention. She studied the sky. Blue.

Maybe it's nothing. Her thought occurred as she cranked the Tahoe

back on and watched Reese take the front passenger seat after pumping gas, something she had warned him repeatedly not to do, not in Oregon, and not at that gas station, where employees were supposed to pump it and seemed to always get cranky if a customer tried to pump his own fuel. At first, she thought the employee was coming to yell at them. His voice could be heard, even though the Tahoe's windows were up and the engine was revving. Loud. But something made her stop, long enough to hear his anxious announcement as he picked up pace, running toward his own car. She replayed it in her mind before taking off as fast as possible, three dogs bouncing in the passenger bench seat and Serenity coming to a crouching position in the far corner of her crate that they kept in the back of the Tahoe. Her only thoughts. *Fuck.* And then a quick review of the gas station employee's high-pitched announcement: *Tsunami's coming.*

Allie didn't stop hearing the siren until she had worked her way up the mountain range that separated Seaside from Portland. She pictured devastation behind her and knew the only thing that separated them from death was kismet. *It was pure fucking luck, having all the animals loaded, having a full tank of gas, and having the camper already attached.* They were circumstances she didn't announce, but conditions she knew made all the difference in their survival.

Others were scrambling to make it over the steep windy mountain range also, backing traffic up, but no one slowed; instead, everyone kept an even pace. It seemed people pulled over as soon as possible after coming down the last bit of the mountain, probably in an effort to process what had just happened. Allie looked for a place to pull off, somewhere that would accommodate a Tahoe and camper. She knew she needed to comprehend what was going on in as much space as possible.

Parking near a Dairy Queen, another ten minutes down the road, she abandoned her role as the getaway driver for a much-needed break, first turning her attention to Serenity, who was nervously cowered in the corner of her crate, but welcomed being scooped up and held near Allie's heartbeat, before she turned her attention to the dogs, administering each a pet-and-scratch, and then finally, she evaluated Reese's face before speaking.

"What just happened?" She tried to ask calmly, but knew she was almost shouting. "Was there a tsunami?" *Tsunami.* The word triggered her memory, reminding her of a trip two years back, one where her mother had followed them to Crescent City, on the coast of California, but near the Oregon border. She closed her eyes, in an effort to calm down, while recalling how she had climbed up the Battery Point Lighthouse stairs with her mother and Reese, and how they had learned about the 1964 tsunami hitting the coast of Northern California, near the border of Oregon. The lighthouse in Crescent City had survived. *Did Seaside?* She wondered privately, a thought that was disrupted when Reese finally answered her last question.

"I don't know." Reese looked shell-shocked as he slowly answered her. He looked around, absorbing the small parking lot, one overcrowded with cars and people. His thoughts even paid attention to the overflow of vehicles dripping down the sides of Highway 26. *Hundreds.* People simply pulled off the highway, most with the same puzzled look as Reese. "I'm going to ask around." He went in for a hug, noticing the worry in her brown eyes, before walking to a semi-truck that had managed to pull off the side of the highway, and whose driver was currently gathering information using his CB radio.

Allie grabbed her cell phone. No service. She hadn't heard from her mother since their pre-Arctic Ocean Shuttle conversation, a call that lasted almost an hour, even though phone service sometimes made their voices sound like some sort of alien beings. *You sound like an alien.* Allie recalled her mother's words. They had both accepted the fact that clear phone service was not going to happen. *Just be careful Mom,* Allie remembered stating. *Call me when you're done with the shuttle.* And then she recalled her mother's words: *I will. I love you.*

Reese walked back after twenty minutes, long enough for Allie to let the dogs pee along the fence line that separated Dairy Queen from the Still Creek Inn & Lounge. Allie could tell by the look on his face, that it wasn't good news.

"The tsunami hit Seaside pretty hard." He spilled the information that seemed to be the talk inside the Dairy Queen. "A lot of people were caught off guard," he followed up. Then shaking his head, he looked at Allie. She could tell his eyes knew more, so she starred through him until he began to talk again. "Ecuador had *one* of the earthquakes." He hated that he had just used the word *one*, but leaving it out would have been deceptive. He looked at her, trying to judge whether she had picked up on his word choice.

"The quake off the coast of South America did this?" She asked point-blank. And then, "One?" The short question was confirmation that she had picked up on the three-letter word. He knew beating around the bush any longer was just going to piss her off. She was too smart for games.

"The trucker I talked to out front said that a quake off the coast of Anchorage sent the tsunami to Oregon." He had no choice but to tell her. He knew she was thinking of her mother on the Dalton, so he wanted to clarify the location once again. "The epicenter was somewhere near the Aleutian Islands."

"Would that affect my mother?" Allie asked the question she was most concerned about.

"No Allie." He took a breath. "There is a big power grid out. Parts of the Pacific Northwest might not have electric or phone service for a week, but that's it." Reese reached for the front passenger car door where they had been standing, signaling that he would drive the rest of the evening, and offering her a chance to co-pilot, something he hoped would distract her. He knew her thoughts were preoccupied.

"Wouldn't most of Alaska be affected?" He could tell by the way she slowly settled into the Tahoe, that her body was craving the worse possible scenario, so he gave it to her.

"It might affect some of the roads as she works her way out of Alaska, but she's way above the epicenter right now, so I'm sure she's fine." He watched her try to suck back in any worry. "She might not even know it happened." He added.

"I guess you're right." Then she thought about how her mother promised to call after getting off the Arctic Ocean Shuttle. "But she hasn't called."

"You don't know that." He said. "Cell phone towers are out everywhere up and down the coast and into Alaska." He reasoned, before adding additional reassurance. "She's probably tried and just thinks service is bad." He answered her honestly, and he hoped his straightforward approach was putting her at ease.

"Maybe you're right." She said. "Let's get out of here," Reese replied by driving the Tahoe and camper toward the parking lot exit, but before he could master turning left on Highway 26, Allie's plea filled the inside of the Tahoe. "Stop." Allie motioned him to pull to the side. Too many people were gathering around the semi-truck driver, the same one that had spent almost twenty minutes sharing information with Reese, so it was obvious new information was being shared.

"He's probably telling everyone what we already found out." Reese noticed Allie's brown eyes studying the growing crowd of people.

"No, it's something more." She felt it in her gut. "Lock the car." She had already exited the passenger side, and with a determined look she was making her way on foot toward the crowd. Reese followed, leaving the dogs inside the locked vehicle. "Something else has happened." She saw the look of panic on people's faces. They approached the crowd, listening for clues. One woman dropped to her knees and began praying out loud.

"Dear Heavenly Father, please protect the children and spare the righteous." Allie knew the woman's useless prayer was more than a delayed reaction to the Seaside tsunami. *Something more.* She told herself again.

"What's going on?" She wasn't asking the elderly woman who was still knelt in prayer; she was asking the middle-aged man who stood beside her, his eyes open, soaking in the information that had passed through the crowd.

"There was just a third earthquake, and a second tsunami." The man said to Allie, and before she could ask where, he continued. "My mother believes the end of the world is coming." Allie noticed his hand touching the shoulder of the woman knelt in prayer.

"Where?" Allie wanted answers. She didn't have time to tread lightly around the religious bullshit that was playing out in front of her.

"Africa." The man's one-word answer seemed insensitive and unfriendly, so he tried to add more, just in case his mother was right, and just in case judgment day was approaching faster than he expected. "My mother believes the truck driver was sent to our location by God to inform us. He's an angel."

"Maybe he's able to inform us because he has a fucking satellite phone and CB Radio." Allie's rebuttal was meant to get the man's attention. "Where in Africa?" She watched the man's lips move but wasn't able to process any words that were spoken; instead, her mind played a short movie, one showing the last evening she had spent with her brother – just a couple of hours together, long enough to introduce him to Reese, and long enough to make off-the-wall jokes about people who were already drunk inside the small Little Rock bar, before the band on stage opened with their first song. She felt like she was hovering above her own body, as she watched the three of them drink down a round of beers and smoke cigarettes at the Four Quarter Bar. While watching the man's lips move, she listened to the lyrics through thick bar smoke. *When the devil comes in makeup boys, we run.* Allie thought about running, but her legs felt faint, and her breathing was too unsteady.

Reese steadied her, then thanked the man, before helping Allie back to the passenger side of the Tahoe. She sat, dazed and confused, until Reese pulled out onto the main road, then her mind cleared, long enough for her to resume questioning, this time with Reese.

"Where did he say the third quake was?" She asked the question as Reese left the crowd of people in his rearview.

"The third quake was by the Horn of Africa, which resulted in a second tsunami." There, he said it.

Allie was quiet for a minute, as her mind evaluated his word choice once again. *Horn of Africa.* She knew he wouldn't call it that, unless he was trying to avoid saying Somalia, her brother's last known whereabouts. Her face fought to hold in all emotion. Reese could tell by the way her eyebrows moved that she was working to process everything, so he remained quiet, allowing her to speak, while he concentrated on the vehicles in front of him.

"Somalia?" She asked.

"Nothing is verified." Reese stated, then continued, "I'm not sure if the information the man stated is correct." He kept his eyes forward, hoping Allie would follow suit, taking the position as co-pilot, and giving him advice on what direction to drive.

"What information did he give?" Allie hadn't heard anything except the raspy voice of the singer who growled out the lyrics inside the Little Rock bar.

"Somalia. 8.3. Tsunami followed."

Allie pointed to the right-hard lane. Reese obliged. They would be in Portland before total darkness surrounded them.

CHAPTER FOUR

ALASKA

No service. Enola May Starks thought the words as she reached her Jeep with Miles around 7:00 that evening, after returning on the Arctic Ocean Shuttle to Deadhorse. Not having cell service wasn't a big surprise. It had been spotty the entire trip, especially on the Dalton. She was as far north as she could drive in Alaska. She had spent the last twenty-four days making her way from Spokane to Deadhorse, first stopping to share two nights with Allie and Reese, who had agreed to meet her near the Washington border, along the Columbia River Gorge, one of Enola's favorite spots, not one of Allie and Reese's usual hangouts, but definitely one of their favorites too. Lately their usual hangout was Seaside, Oregon, a place that Reese and Allie were considering staying for a while. Enola had visited them there during Mother's Day and could understand why Seaside would appeal to them. The smell of the Pacific stayed in the air. Elk and American Bald Eagles made the small ocean town their home. It was small enough to have breathing room from the masses, but large enough to find jobs. Still, like Enola, Allie wasn't ready to settle, and jumped at the opportunity to meet her mother at the Oregon-Washington border for a few days.

"Only two nights," Enola said to Allie. "I want to be in Alaska for my birthday." Normally, Enola would want her birthday to be as close to Allie as possible, but this time she needed to prove that turning fifty-eight didn't lessen her strength and resilience. Driving from Washington State to Alaska wasn't for the weak-minded. There were a lot of windy, long roads stretching through British Columbia and The Yukon, before Alaska became a reality.

"I have no doubt you will Mom," Allie spoke up. She knew her mother's age wasn't deteriorating any part of the woman she admired. Nonetheless, it was hard to say goodbye the morning her mother pulled away from the camp spot they had shared. "I'll miss you." She hugged Enola long and hard. "Call, text, email." She smiled before handing Enola a box the size of her hand. "Don't open this until you're in Alaska for your birthday."

"I promise." Enola was fighting back tears. Being brave didn't include saying goodbye to Allie. "I love you with all of my heart." She took the box, but not before hugging Allie with both arms one last time.

"We had cell service before we got on the shuttle," Enola said to Miles. He wagged his tail, a friendly gesture, but Enola could tell he was on high alert, examining his surroundings. His eyes seemed to study the Jeep's appearance, a chalky dried mud had permanently replaced the factory painted bright red, or so it seemed, as it had become part of the Jeep's new look over the last five days, a sign that it had driven the unforgiving 414 mile-stretch of gravel and dirt surfaced road. "It's okay Miles," Enola reassured him, as she opened the driver's door, allowing Miles to make his way to his co-pilot platform, constructed out of two plastic food bins, and topped with a dog bed, one that placed him level with the window, giving him a bird's eye view of everything. He hopped in when signaled, taking his co-pilot position, as Enola slowly pulled away from The Deadhorse Camp, a graveyard of scrap metal, oil company machinery, and empty semitrailers that were propped open. She pointed her muddy Jeep in the direction of open tundra. The rain came down before she even made ten miles, and its accomplice – wind – joined in, making the attempt to drive the Dalton more challenging. Enola studied the gray sky and bitter cold setting in around her, as she bounced from one muddy pothole to another. She was thirty minutes into her drive when she noticed two dropped cargo trailers. Each one had been dropped by a semi-truck – one green, one orange – and both locked uptight. *Had a couple of semi-truck drivers simply abandoned their load?* She pondered her silent question. Before she could come up with a good answer for abandoning cargo on the side of the road, she passed a metal cross on the right side of the Dalton, its middle decorated with ribbon and plastic flowers. *Maybe the weather is too bad to continue?* She questioned, knowing drivers had died on the Dalton, and knowing that their companies took every precaution to protect them. A large gust of wind blew Enola's Jeep, pushing her vehicle to the left-hand side of the road, at least a good foot. *Maybe,* she thought. *Maybe the drivers knew each other, decided to unhook their loads due to high winds and decided to travel into Deadhorse for a good night's sleep.* It was a theory that made sense to her. *They'll return in the morning for their loads.* Her thoughts settled, then after one additional thought she continued. *Forward.* Enola could hear Dixie's sweet voice speak the word softly, urging Enola to keep going in her travels. It was a memory that stayed with her as she continued to drive. The rain slowed, allowing Enola to study the crevices throughout the landscape. *That's what the shuttle driver was talking about.* She told herself, as she studied the terrain, topography once filled with streams of free-flowing water, were now filled with Alaskan foliage – deceptive areas according to the shuttle driver. *You'll sink in thigh-deep in some of those areas.* She recalled him mentioning. Dark olive greens, blood red, and golden yellow hid the mushy traps that waited for innocent hikers and animals.

Her eyes left the landscape and searched the sky, where she noticed a huge seagull keeping pace with her driver's side, a sight that almost caused Enola to miss mile marker 368, a location that held clues for another possible theory about the abandoned cargo. There she noticed one small red and white plane, with N56456 clearly painted near the pilot's door. This time it was parked alone, unaccompanied by the other two single-engine planes she had noticed on the way up the Dalton. *Maybe the truckers flew out for another job.* She told herself, before trying to convince Miles.

"We're going to be okay," Enola reassured him in a calming voice, as she deciphered the look on his face, one that matched the bumpy ride five days earlier, when they had made their way up the Dalton, and one that had taken them four full days to travel from Livengood, much of it a steep narrow climb, some with no guardrails.

"We've got this Miles." She said out loud. "We're the masters of off-road driving." She was referring to her life – and his.

He seemed to give her a look that meant he was in total agreeance. That was all she needed. She continued to point her Jeep south on Dalton Highway. She drove, unaware that the desolate gravel road, full of potholes and rough terrain, was nothing compared to where they were heading. Behind her, the earthquake was *now* the talk of Deadhorse. Word had finally spread. Truckers were notified by CB radio not to head south due to fuel shortage and dangerous driving conditions. Just wait. That was the instruction given. Of course, Enola had no way of knowing, and she was already making her way down the Dalton, although slowly.

The gravel crunched as Enola made her way south. It was nearly 500 miles back to Fairbanks, the first 414 of that on Dalton Highway, at least fifty of which she wanted to accomplish tonight. She imagined that most of the stretch would be alone, like it had been on her trip up, but she welcomed the silence. Even on a bumpy road, the world around her seemed tranquil. For a few minutes, she graciously maneuvered on a rare stretch of battered asphalt, one where her eyes kept watch, knowing that a pothole in the seven or eight-mile track of intermittently paved road wouldn't be as forgiving on her tires as the surface that surrounded a dirt pothole.

The thermometer gauge inside her Jeep started to plunge. Slowly. Forty-three. Forty-one. Thirty-nine. She knew sleeping in a higher altitude meant lower temps. "Let's stop here." She knew it was the last valley she would see for a while. Pulling over, she positioned her vehicle near the pipeline. The cold raced her as she walked from one side of her car to another, first to collect a small cooking pot from a plastic container underneath Miles' high-rise, then her one-burner stove with the propane cylinder that fit nicely into its base from the vehicle's right floor, followed by a lighter, a jug of water, one chicken Cup-a-Soup, a pack of Peak dog food, with real beef chunks for Miles, and a can of Vernors Ginger Ale, which, to the touch, was as cold as the inside of a refrigerator. "We'll eat and use the remainder of daylight to get set up." She looked at her co-pilot, his eyes showed appreciation for the routine Enola had established. Find a safe camp spot. Cook. Eat. Sleep.

Enola snuggled beside Miles under several blankets and her thermal sleeping bag, which she had unzipped, spreading it into a full-size blanket. The cold air stung her face, which she allowed for a while, just so she could stare at The Trans-Alaska Pipeline, without anything blocking her vision. She thought about her grandfather, Homer Parrish, and how he worked on the pipeline for three years of his life. For a moment, she felt he was near her, watching over her, in the one a.m. moonlight. Enola didn't believe in heaven or hell, not as real places, but believed her grandfather was out there, somewhere, and was certain that he checked in on her from time to time, just to make sure she was okay. Silently, she spoke to him. *Thanks for letting me live with you during high school. I needed you in my life.* She sobbed. *I miss you, and I'm sorry my mother wasn't able to love you.* Her thoughts shifted to Homer's daughter, her mother, Melantha Fears, a person who went through her life not loving anyone. Then her thoughts moved down the silver pipeline, along with her line of vision, both hidden in the self-made tunnel that had formed out of the thick insulated material nearest her face. It allowed her eyes to focus on the silver snake that lurked just outside her window, its belly full of crude oil, on its way to a refinery.

Through bitter cold, she smiled at the similarities between the crude oil and her convictions, as she imagined her thoughts being separated into useful parts, matching the fate of the petroleum inside the pipeline that slept beside her. *Mitch doesn't want you or Allie in his life.* She told herself. *Was it a trait he inherited from Melantha?* It was a question she didn't want to process, and one that she would never have the answer to anyway.

Pulling the sleeping bag tighter underneath her chin, she watched the far end of the tunnel collapse. Darkness surrounded her. *Separate. Convert. Treat.* It was a process that would be ongoing. The words played over and over in her mind as she drifted off to sleep. *Separate. Convert. Treat.*

CHAPTER FIVE

EIGHT MONTHS EARLIER

Dixie was my constant: always a friend, always full of compassion, and always called me on Christmas. We had been magnets since first grade, since my childhood had been uprooted from Detroit and made its way to the mountains in Asheville, North Carolina. Distance didn't separate us.

"Merry Christmas Sis." I hadn't even said hello before Dixie rattled off her salutation.

"Merry Christmas Dix," I replied. "How's life?" It was a general question, but one I was sorry I had asked, remembering that life had given Dixie stage four cancer nearly two years ago.

"The doctor from Duke Hospital called me yesterday." She took in air before continuing. "He thinks I should do the combination treatment."

"The Yervoy and Opdivo combination?" My voice was steady, as I recalled my research several days earlier, tucked away in a coffee shop, in Los Banos, hidden in the corner with my computer, a small table chosen with care, partially to use the available electrical outlet and partially to hide my tears from other coffeeshop patrons. Crying about Dixie's stage four cancer was something I wanted to do in private. Dixie was a fighter; I knew that, but I was afraid of drugs that had names so long that nicknames had to be used. Yervoy was Ipilimumab and was used to boost the immune system; Opdivo was Nivolumab and was supposed to trick T-cells into recognizing cancer as normal, so that Dixie's immune system could destroy them. I closed my eyes, listening to Dixie on the other end of the phone, imagining the war that was going on inside of her body, and shaking at the thought of the one to come.

"Yes." Dixie stopped talking long enough to gain her composure. "I guess it's my best option." I listened to my friend of fifty-one years talk about stage four cancer, about intravenous treatments, about side effects, about how she wanted more than a fifteen to twenty percent survival rate for living another five years, and about how she wanted more Christmases.

"You're going to beat this Dixie." I choked back tears. I knew Dixie's cancer had already spread to several lymph nodes. I knew the odds. I knew Dixie would have to put up one hell of a fight. "I'm going to see you in the spring," I added in an attempt to give Dixie the only thing that I knew existed – hope. It was the only thing that was real.

"Yes, you will Sis." Dixie blurted back. "I guess I might have to try one of those crazy coffee house drinks with you."

"Deal," I said. "I love you." And then, "Merry Christmas."

"I love you too." Dixie continued talking, first about Ryan, how lucky she was to have him, and how they were going to go to her dad's for Christmas. *Some marriages do last*, I thought as I listened. And then, *Dixie at least deserved that.*

It wasn't until, I said goodbye to Dixie that I realized I had been following Allie and Reese's Tahoe and camper to the San Luis Reservoir. After parking, I let tears and tall strands of golden sea oats blur my view from the inside of my Jeep, where Miles had made his way to my lap to comfort me. I held him tight, pulling away to look at his innocent Detroit butterscotch eyes, before reaching for his leash, and exiting my vehicle. My wet eyes searched for Allie.

"You okay?" She looked at me.

"Dixie." It was a one-word answer, but she knew there was an endless conversation behind it.

"She has to do the combo treatment?" Her question proved she had listened to me ramble, after doing research on my laptop a few days earlier.

"Yes," I said. Nothing more I simply took Allie's hand and looked out at the golden hills that swirled haphazardly to the edge of the reservoir. I imagined beautiful sheets of music, each with semiquavers and minim symbols, performing an illusory dance. The vision gave me strength. *Stay strong.* I thought the words for Dixie, and then after wiping away several more tears, and following Allie and Reese into their camper, I thought the same words for Mitch. *Stay strong.*

Maybe it was nature. Maybe it was watching four dogs and a cat open their Christmas gifts. Or, maybe it was the vision of twirling musical notes that played tricks on my mind, but for a moment, ever so briefly, I let my mind rest. I watched Shiloh hold down present after present with one paw as she pulled wrapping paper off with her teeth. I watched Zeus use both paws and open his gifts without any help. I watched Yoda bounce with excitement as he ripped his gifts open, the first revealing a stuffed opossum. Then I watched Miles. He guarded his mound, each present wrapped in bright red tissue paper, until the other dogs were distracted with gifts of their own, then he started to rip each open: first a red and white stuffed Santa Claus' head from Allie, then a bright green tennis ball from Reese, and finally a large rawhide from me. Serenity scurried around each four-legged canine, chasing catnip that taunted her, hidden inside a bright orange mouse body.

I looked around inside their camper. They had little of value: a daybed, a two-burner propane stove, a crate with cooking supplies, another with dog supplies, and miscellaneous items that helped them survive everyday life. They seemed to have nothing in a camper that was in desperate need of repair, but they had everything – smiles, laughter, and unconditional love for each other. I couldn't judge their lifestyle, even though I wanted to. Sure, I didn't like that my daughter was living day-to-day, but somewhere in those Narducci' brown eyes, there was something priceless. She didn't live her life by society's standards. She lived each day like it was her last – loving, traveling, touching nature, and yearning for more. Every time I looked at her, she sparkled. Her laughter fell like snowflakes in the surrounding Diablo Range, a ribbon of mountains and rolling hills, that captured our attention around the reservoir, as the evening sky turned into bright reds, playful blues, earthy greens and sunshine yellow. I tried my best to capture Allie's spirit in several snapshots: one of the three of us standing with our backs to the melting sky, one of just Allie and me, cheek to cheek, our figures only silhouettes, and a secret snapshot of just Allie, as she turned to face the western slopes, her long hair hiding her shoulder blades, and her back unaware of my admiring eyes. It was then, in that very moment, that I realized she couldn't be captured, only loved. The list of similarities between us was longer than I wanted to admit.

Christmas night, I savored each bite of the meal Reese and Allie had prepared, a smorgasbord: steaks, cheese ravioli, garlic buttered shrimp, asparagus, mashed potatoes, stuffing, and gravy. Candlelight and laughter accompanied conversation and tears, especially when I confessed my concerns over not hearing from Mitch for a second Christmas. Somehow Allie put things in perspective. *People are who they are.* It was a simple observation, but one I needed to remember. I would always love him, but I was done chasing people that didn't want to be part of my life, including my own son. That was another aha moment for me, one where as a mother, I finally accepted that the souls I gave birth to are not mine to keep.

I looked across the room at Allie. Her smile sparkled even in the dim lighting. It radiated my soul and reminded me that I must have done something right in a world where I had often felt punished. *Life doesn't give you what you deserve.* I reminded myself again. *You have to use what you have.* I sat there, silently analyzing the statements I had said so many times privately. *I deserved loving parents. I deserved an adult son whose loyalty and love would follow me into my elderly years. I deserved a husband who loved me for my essence and strength. I didn't get unconditional love from those people.* My thoughts stopped, as they reorganized and refocused on what I did get. *I have an adult daughter whose love shines warmth and light on me every day of my life. I have my health, my wisdom, my courage, and my strength. Standing alone was something I could do without compromise.* I took a deep breath.

"Merry Christmas Allie and Reese." Looking into the four eyes that looked at me, I watched a galaxy unfold before me.

CHAPTER SIX

SOMALIA

Paul Wabel's face froze in stunned silence, as he sat in his office chair, a spot where he had planted himself for the last three hours, studying graphs and charts, blueprints that supplied evidence-based activity that had occurred within and around Mount Spurr, the stratovolcano in the Aleutian Arc of Alaska, and Guagua Pichincha, another stratovolcano, and one known as Ecuador's giant, with a diameter of over fourteen miles. Paul had a lot of respect for both towering volcanoes, their bellies made of lava and ash, and felt like a proud father, having both of them in his Ring of Fire.

Listening to a third report print, he took notice immediately. *Someone else's child.* The thought settled him, as his eyes followed the dark printout containing angry-looking lines. Still, he was having a hard time accepting the fact that three major earthquakes had occurred just in the last three and a half hours. Examining the newest report, he audited the severity of the earthquake that had just taken place off the northeast coast of Africa, a location approximately a third of the way around the world. Disaster's reach was infinite. Somalia had been hit hard.

The Gulf of Aden had collided with the Red Sea, a head-on collision, pulling unsuspecting members of the small East African community off their feet. It was already Thursday in Somalia, just after six a.m., an eleven-hour time difference from Anchorage's current time of 7:05 p.m. Paul's eyes widened, as he looked over the graphic charts at his fingertips, comparing the three different Richter scales. *Logarithm base ten with an exponent of seven.* He placed it behind the other two reports. *Another, logarithm base ten with an exponent of seven.* His right hand slid the second report into third

position, while his mind categorized the first two quakes. *Strong.*

Then, he stared at the third printout. *Fuck.* He thought. *Base ten*

eight. And then, *major.* He closed his eyes, trying not to think of the

devastation. He knew it was the result of tectonic plates, crustal

plates that usually performed as a well-oiled machine, but like all

machines, had malfunctioned. Again. He knew there had been over

two dozen significant earthquakes near Somalia in the last four

years, and a serious earthquake in the Indian Ocean, which twelve

years ago left the community with over 50,000 homeless people,

hundreds dead, and entire villages swept away, most a result of the

tsunami that followed. Now, once again, the African and Arabian

plate boundaries were at war. Like an abusive relationship, they had

made unacceptable physical contact, invading each other's personal

space, and promoting friction and stress that wasn't able to be

contained any longer. The punch was lethal, something he imagined

just as his satellite phone signaled an incoming call. Another one.

This time it was from a well-known news station in West Palm

Beach, Florida.

"Paul, this is David Covack, West Palm Beach." He paused. "A pretty big quake just hit the horn of Africa." He made the announcement as a formality, his intention set on gathering information. "Is Nyamuragira responsible?" He asked, referring to one of the world's most active volcanoes.

"Hey David, I'm looking at the printout now." He held the one-page computerized document in his right hand and his satellite phone with his left. "It's not one of my babies; although, I am aware that Nyamuragira has a lot of molten rock underneath it. I'm also aware that a lot of people believe volcanoes trigger earthquakes." Then, after pausing, he reiterated the same thing he had been saying phone call after phone call, for over three hours without much of a break. "Volcanic swarms will not cause a quake."

"Just checking to see what you knew." David Covack, *a fucking meteorologist*, *nothing more*, repetitive thoughts echoed in Paul's mind as he listened to Covack make one more final statement before hanging up the phone in his West Palm Beach office. "It doesn't feel right having three major quakes and two major tsunamis within a four-hour time stretch."

I'm not responsible for every goddamn quake and tsunami that occurs around the globe. It was Paul's last thought before disconnecting from the east coast of Florida, but not his last for the evening. He reached for the tsunami printout, one that he had noticed, but refrained from grabbing earlier. *A fucking war zone 8000 miles away.*

The sun wasn't fully awake when the earthquake and tsunami hit Somalia, but the coastline was already in full operation, some villagers had already started removing fish, squid, and large shrimp from boat-wells, others were cleaning fishing boats that had just docked following their all-night excursions at sea, and dozens of women in the small fishing community were standing with their backs to the still darkened, but early morning skyline. Holding baskets of produce they had grown in their own gardens and goat cheese they had made by boiling goat milk and vinegar until it formed large curds, which they carefully wrapped in valued cheesecloth overnight, they were ready to trade their goods for a basket of fresh seafood for their families. It was an early morning process that occurred while small children were still sleeping, and while school-age children started their morning chores, first gathering wood for a fire, so moms could get breakfast started when they returned with a mixture of fresh seafood – some that would be immediately used to made seafood pancakes, or a bread pocket filled with fish, or a breakfast bowl, (usually with onion, leafy vegetables from the family garden, coconut, and shrimp), then to search the early morning shoreline for needed supplies requested by the matriarch (often a large shell that could be used for dipping sauces and serving rice, three or four strands of seaweed to season planned family meals, or hunt down the occasional request for bullwhip to make medicine or provide extra nourishment in broth that yearned for substantial ingredients). They were duties that needed to be completed within the first hour of daylight, in order to have first dibs on items that had washed up during the night from the Indian Ocean.

When the earth shook the edge of the coastal community, at least two dozen women were walking on the shoreline, each carrying a small basket of mixed seafood, after deals were made and goods were exchanged, leaving them walking miles along the coastal community back to their makeshift huts. One woman, Maryam, spotted her son Sahib, as he reached for a large conch shell, just as the quake struck.

"Earthquake!" Mitch shouted from the shoreline. His voice was overpowered by the sound of poorly built houses crashing to the ground and screams from women and young teens up and down the coastline. Mitch's blue eyes, the same ones Enola's mother once flaunted to get whatever she wanted, absorbed the scurry of villagers, and the toppling over of family huts and thriving storefronts that gave the area a sense of community.

Luckily, Mitch's eyes noticed the receding water level, something that occurred quickly, leaving a void where the Gulf of Aden normally touched the Indian Ocean. It was as if someone sucked all the water out with a big straw, leaving fishing boats that had rocked minutes earlier in the untamed body of water nearly grounded. *Tsunami.* That was his first thought, before he turned to run as fast as he could, the early morning sunrise at his back. His legs moved faster than any thoughts that followed. *Highlands.* He could hear the rush of unstoppable water behind him.

#

Somalia was on the east side of the Great Rift Valley and was made up of hidden fault lines and dramatically different elevation levels. By all appearances, it was paradise, until closer observation, then it replicated Hades, a final destination for lost souls. The volcanoes that towered in the backdrop of Somalia were seldom explored by mankind; instead, they served as hiding spots for cheetahs, gorillas, and lions. Humans sometimes became prey. Quick. Easy. And those that managed to survive for a short period of time were usually faced with other life-threatening challenges: no water, death trapping crevices in the earth's surface, and disease, mostly from mosquitoes or other insects. Villagers knew what Mitch knew, if you want to survive stay close to the villages along the Gulf of Aden and the Indian Ocean. But now, that wasn't a choice. Everyone who was alive was running toward the highlands. A wall of water, its height equal to that of a football field, showed no mercy to the small village just north of Mogadishu, flattening everything in its path, and pulling homes that were still standing off their foundations, like bad teeth. A fist with a 360-foot surface annihilated the village.

A young boy, eight years old, with dark eyes, almost black in color, reached for Mitch's hand, his own letting go of the large shell he had just collected for his mother, one perfect for holding the rice she cooked with most meals. His other hand held a shiny piece of abalone, which he planned on making into a necklace for his mother, Maryam. Now, his small legs moved as quickly as possible in an effort to keep up. Out of his peripheral vision, Mitch saw people and livestock being tossed about in the solid block of water which seemed to almost touch him. Without a second to spare, Mitch reached a deep ravine, and without a moment's thought, he did the only thing he knew to do.

"Jump." It was non-negotiable, as he was still holding the hand of Sahib, a boy he recognized as the son of a local fisherman that he had met a couple years back, on the coast of Somalia, near Mogadishu.

Not knowing what was in the body of water below him was the least of Mitch's worries. He was more concerned with the wall of water at his back. It seemed like the longest jump in history, and after realizing the river was deeper than he expected, he accepted the fact that he was dead, but only for a few seconds. When he heard Sahib's rattling cough, he propelled his body to the surface, where he managed to kick his booted feet in the Shebelle River, staying afloat long enough to pull Sahib to his side, in the early morning light.

A graveyard of dead tsetse flies surrounded them, their tiny legs and arms crossed, signaling their demise; still, Mitch knew that seeing so many dead tsetse flies was a sign that there were just as many live ones, which fueled his exit to the northeastern riverbank.

Sahib had seen their devastation first hand, had seen the bite on his father's neck, had watched his mother place a wet cloth on his father's forehead, as he writhed in pain from fever and muscles that felt squeezed. The young boy's mother, Maryam, had spent endless hours helping her husband, his final months full of confusion and barely able to stand, until one day he lay down, falling into a permanent sleep. Sahib was six. Now, two years later, he wondered if he'd ever see his mother, Maryam, again. He placed his hands, one of which still miraculously cupped the piece of abalone, over his eyes and begin to cry, as his feet worked to tread the muddy path along the Shebelle River, until he felt Mitch grab his empty hand and pull.

"Sahib, come on." Mitch's voice was authoritative and had little room for emotion.

"Hooyo." Sahib knew English, because of his father, but cried out the word *mother* in Somalian. It had been hard enough losing his father, the man who taught him how to speak a little English, a little Swahili, and a little Oromo. His father, Kwamboka, was from Kenya, and believed knowing other languages increased the prospect of trading goods along the Indian Ocean. For Kwamboka, it did. He was able to feed his family, and even after his death, the shillings that had been squirreled away, kept Sahib and Maryam fed. Now, there was nothing left. And, Sahib's last memory of his mother, one where she screamed his name, just as a wave sandwiched her between the side of a building and an old truck, left him with a handful of words she had taught him in Somali, her native language, and a shiny piece of abalone that he would never be able to give her.

"We don't have time for that now!" Screamed Mitch, his leather boots in a constant fight with the swelling river that had taken on a large portion of the Indian Ocean, and his mind in a constant fight with the decision to discontinue all contact with his own mother, Enola, and his sister Allie.

"Mother." Sahib voiced his concern in English.

"We have to keep moving." Mitch's boots struggled in thick mud, as he pulled Sahib by the hand, while making his way along the bank of the river, which seemed to still be chasing them. "Let's find someplace safe to wait this out, away from all these damn bugs."

Sahib knew enough English to communicate with Mitch, especially the word *bug*.

"Bug kill father," Sahib informed the hand that pulled him.

"I know Sahib." He said panting. "I used to work with your father."

His eyes searched the highlands. *A cave.* It would be a long treacherous climb, maybe a couple of hours, but would get them above the rising water, and out of the storm that was filling the morning sky, one that had turned from early sunlight to gray and cloudy. He released the hand he had been holding, and used both of his own to clear the thick brush that separated him from the cave about two hundred feet straight up. It would be a hard climb, but one Mitch wanted to make. He wanted to be clear of rising water levels and away from the elements, and he knew being inside a cave was their best chance at survival, at least until they were able to go back to the village. They were both already soaking wet, and within the next two hours, they would be fighting the biting cold that accompanied Africa's monsoon-type rainstorms.

Living on the coast of Africa had increased his knowledge about the area, and he had used that knowledge over the last couple of years to figure out how it could help him in a survival situation. Now, he was glad he had learned about soapstone, something an elder in the community had taught him how to heat for warmth, and had even shared his opinion on where to best discover soapstone. *Caves.* Mitch remembered the wrinkled face explaining.

Aftershocks shook the ground, as Mitch made his way up the steep incline toward the cave. He grabbed at lose pieces of wood and broken limbs as he made his way through the thick foliage, handing small pieces to Sahib.

"Carry this for fire." His instruction was short as he picked up pace, one hand fighting to clear the path, and the other stopping long enough to pick up a decent-sized branch. "Keep up." He snapped.

Reaching the cave, Mitch entered cautiously, checking to make sure it was safe. It wasn't very deep, which he preferred, and had several hand-size pieces of soapstone near the walls and scattered throughout the cave's flooring, just like the elderly villager had told Mitch.

Unsure, how much fluid was left in the only lighter he owned, one hanging on a lanyard just inside his shirt, he carefully placed the largest piece of wood on top of a nest of small tinder that Sahib had been carrying. He didn't know how many chances he would have to light the tee-pee constructed structure before his lighter was just a memory of the world he left behind. One. Two. Nothing. *Maybe it's too wet*, he thought before allowing his thumb to grasp the spark wheel once again. Three. Four. Five. Finally.

Light. Blow. Smoke. Flame. Fire. He kissed the lucky lighter, which he kept cupped in one hand, before slipping the empty green lanyard that normally held it back over his neck, and before instructing Sahib to gather soapstone.

"Four pieces." He pointed. "This size." He held out the palm of his hand, making a circle around its edge with the hand that still held his lucky lighter, one he had purchased in New York, before boarding a tanker that would take him away from his life in America. Looking at the lighter, he flicked the spark wheel one last time. Nothing. Again. Nothing. Again. Nothing. It was empty now, like his emotions. "Drop that damn shell." He barked. "And take off your shoes and socks and most of your clothing," Mitch instructed. Sahib followed Mitch's example, placing his socks close to the backside of the fire, along with his pants. Leaving on his underwear and shirt, he moved close to the front side of the fire where the rocks were heating. The flame worked to heat the rocks and clothing that were scattered behind it, as well as the shirts that sat before it. Complete silence filled the cave.

One hour later, Mitch used his socks and the socks of his accomplice, to pick up one rock at a time, and drop each one into the toe of the empty sock. Handing Sahib back his own two, he instructed him to curl up close to the dying fire with one heated rock tucked under his nearly dry shirt, and the other cradled in his hands.

He watched Sahib's eyes close, as his eight-year-old body absorbed the warmth from the soapstone, and he gave into a noon nap, while he busied his own hands, first by tossing his empty lighter into the fire, where he watched the casing melt into a blackened and deformed mass of plastic, all before reaching for the shiny piece of abalone, which he worked to securely tie to the lanyard that hung empty around his neck.

Removing the refurbished lanyard, a nylon thread to his past, he positioned it beside Sahib, while his mind tried not to care about motherless boys.

CHAPTER SEVEN

SEVEN MONTHS EARLIER

By time I reached Arizona, my entire camper had been repainted red with white trim on the doors and black trim on the sections of crisscrossed aluminum, and I knew 2019 was going to be one thing – different. How, I wasn't sure yet, but I knew my current thought was about Dixie, so I dialed.

"How was the first week of the year for you Sis?" I questioned. "Any complaints?" I tried to be *our* normal, not wanting to make her feel like everything was about the C-word that she was living with day in and day out.

"Yes, it's cold here." Then she added. "Twenty-six, but I've got the heat turned up."

"Mid-forties in Phoenix." I declared. "No heat in my camper, but I'm under four blankets with Miles right beside me, so I don't feel it."

"Just don't get up." She laughed.

"I know, right?" I asked rhetorically.

"I miss you." Dixie started. "I can't wait to see you this spring." Then she followed up. "Take your time. The roads still have a layer of ice on them. People will be sliding everywhere for the next couple of months."

Dixie's voice grew tired after talking about new places in Asheville for us to shop, about her dogs, Kobie and Josie, and about how years move faster with age. I could hear defeat in her voice. *Keep fighting Dixie.* I thought the words, but didn't say them before exchanging goodbyes. A silence followed, which seemed to last longer than usual, as I kept my thoughts on Dixie, until I realized my cell phone was ringing. I answered.

"Hey Mom." It was Allie. I could hear Kitty Forman's high-pitched voice from reruns of *That '70s Show* on their new television that Reese had mounted on the sturdiest wall in their camper. *A car is not a bedroom on wheels.* I processed the ironic humor in Kitty Forman's declaration, and privately snickered.

"We're settled back in Seaside," Allie announced. "How's 2019 treating you so far?"

"Living the dream." I chuckled. Then, "I love you." I felt it in every fiber of my body. There wasn't a day that went by, since she had turned eighteen, and since she had moved away from home, that I didn't want her to come back, didn't want her to go to college and live at home, and didn't want her smile and deep chocolate eyes to be something I saw every day. Now, she was over 1400 miles away, something that would grow as I traveled closer to Dixie. "I'm glad you're back at the campground you like in Seaside," I added, before listening to Allie talk about how Yoda and Shiloh had become best buddies.

"Shiloh knows that's her baby." Allie was referring to Yoda, the returned puppy, who was already over one-year-old.

"Moms never forget," I said, feeling the absence for both Allie and Mitch, even though I was working to let one go who preferred it that way, and let one go who needed it to be that way. For a moment, I thought about the cruelty of having offspring, a being that comes out of your own body, but one you eventually have to give to the universe. "I'm sure she likes having one of her puppies back." I tried not to laugh, thinking of the similarities. *One puppy. One child.* Realizing the thought was a silly comparison, I let it go; although, I was jealous that Shiloh had one of hers near her every day.

"I hope the others are happy " Allie had a hard time letting go also.

"They are," I reassured her, imagining it was something her soul needed, just as mine needed reassurance. A phone call or text works magic when adult children are elsewhere. It's the not knowing that hurts. "You gave them to great homes," I added.

"I love you Mom." *Magical words,* I thought. *Priceless.*

"I love you too, Allie."

"What city are you headed to next?" She asked.

"Tucson." I eyed a folded map that I kept above the visor, although I rarely used it. Garmin GPS kept me straight, a gift from Dixie. *Forward.* I recalled her statement when she gave it to me.

"Well, be careful." She announced with slight worry in her voice.

"Always," I said. "You be careful."

"Mom, it's Seaside." She laughed. "Nothing bad ever happens here."

"Just be careful." My motherly instincts kicked in, even though I knew what she meant. Seaside had small roads, friendly people, and low crime. "Don't ever forget I love you," I said before hearing her say it to me one more time.

Distance grew and days rolled into each other, as well as places. I don't remember deciding to leave Phoenix. I only remember spending a second week in Tucson, another desert oasis, only different. This one had mountains that reminded me of Spokane. I sat my cruise control on twenty-five miles an hour and watched the elevation climb as I wiggled my way up Mount Lemmon like a snake. At the top, I pulled over, letting Miles play in a bank of leftover snow and ice, where he'd scoop up large mouthfuls, in his downward-facing dog pose, which signaled gratefulness to the rest of the world.

Tucson turned into Willcox, where during my third night there, Katy the owner of a roadside food stand, wrapped my hotdog in bacon and topped it with mustard, guacamole, peppers, homemade pinto beans, mayonnaise, onions, tomato, and jalapeno sauce. Each bite enthusiastically made its way to my taste buds, satisfying my craving for salt, sweets, and meat. *Umami.* My mind remembered how *meat* became an official taste in the 1980s; it was a decade when people appreciated the taste of monosodium glutamate, a salty characteristic, and now a taste some steer clear of. The comparison made me think of Mitch, born the same decade, known to be salty, often agitated and angry, and like Umami, most overlooked his fundamental goodness.

I went to sleep that night missing my adult son.

Driving before the sun reached six a.m. the next morning, I made Las Cruces by three in the afternoon. There was something I liked about New Mexico. Maybe it was the way the sun disappeared into the flattest part of the earth. Maybe it was the hidden secrets in the desert, an occasional rabbit or deer track that teased me to keep moving forward, or maybe it was the fact that it felt so alone, but still managed to survive the test of time.

Las Cruces was just as poor as every other desert town. Street corners held the homeless. Cardboard signs were displayed in hand on both sides of the road. *Anything helps.* I replayed the thirty-something woman's sign as I drove by. My window was down just enough to hear her frustration when I didn't stop to give her money. *Fuck you.* I let her words dance in my head without reacting.

Weaving past the center of town, I regained speed, but slowed when I noticed a cemetery off to my passenger side. Miles sat tall, his nose out the window. *Sniff.* Dirt rolled in. I could tell by the way he pulled his face to safety. It was the first cemetery I had ever seen that looked so lifeless. I laughed at my thoughts. *Aren't they all lifeless?* I questioned. But there was something different about this one. No grass. No color. No flowers. No visitors. Nothing. Plain. Except for scattered trash here and there, the cemetery stood like a ghost town on Grigg's Street. I pulled my car and trailer to a stop off the side of the road, letting others pass. I got out and made my way to the edge of the sidewalk, examining the fate of over thirty people I quickly calculated. Some graves were marked with cinder blocks, some with wooden crosses, and one or two with aluminum markers. The scene sent a chill down my neck. Miles alerted me with a single bark that a man was approaching, his feet pulling the wheelchair he was seated in. Slowly. He smiled a weathered, nearly toothless smile.

"Hello," I said as he rolled closer.

"Good day." He said, wanting my attention. "Do you know someone in there?" He asked.

"No," I answered, wondering if he did.

"It's a sad sight." He said. "I guess I'll end up there someday soon." His tone was serious.

"Why is it so . . ." I searched for the word, "plain?" I knew that wasn't the word I wanted. *Undecorated?* I privately corrected my thoughts.

"It's for poor people." He informed me as he wheeled another three or four inches closer. "Those people don't have any family." He had no emotion in his voice. "They're like me."

"I'm sorry." I didn't know what else to say to the wheelchair-bound face, leathered by the New Mexico sun.

"It's okay." He said. "I'm used to it." I noticed three teeth when he smiled. One hidden in the top left, and two on the bottom. Surely there were more in back, I imagined, as I contemplated how difficult it must be to eat.

"I don't have a lot of family either." I tried to say something that showed empathy.

"We all end up in the same place eventually." He said with all three teeth exposed.

"Where's that?" I asked him, hoping he really did have the answer.

"There." He pointed toward the sky. Long streams of white puffy cloud mass filled the sky overhead. "They're not clouds," he announced. "They're spirits." That's when he couldn't stop talking. He told me his father and mother were both Chiricahua Indians and that they were buried in the New Mexico desert in unmarked graves with no coffins or chemicals used in their bodies after death. He explained how their spirits are on a journey, again pointing up. "It's not sad," he explained as he continued to tell me about how he was going to soar during his journey. "It's an adventure." He smiled, this time with his heart.

I bent over to hug him, not because he needed it, but because I did. I wanted to believe death wasn't the end. *It's a cycle.* I recalled him saying as I drove away. *It never ends.* The wise man's voice soothed me as I made my way back to I-10; I traveled west, but only for a few minutes, just long enough to make my way to the Recycled Roadrunner Scenic View Rest Stop, where after pulling in, I angled my car and camper along the top of the plateau, so that I would have a great view of Las Cruces. Below, I could see street lights in the daylight that were just starting to fade. Above, I watched a crystallized and frozen water-world move slowly over the city, as the sun melted into the western sky behind me. *Spirits.* I thought.

CHAPTER EIGHT

ECUADOR

Paul Wabel turned on the small satellite television, located near the end of his office sofa, the one he planned to make his home for the night. It had been a long day, one where he had spent several hours studying printouts and answering incoming calls, some about the quake off the coast of Anchorage, a few about the quake off Somalia, and over the last thirty minutes, several calls concerning the quake off the coast of Ecuador.

Now, he was stretched out on the brown leather sofa, watching a prerecorded satellite news report about the quake that had occurred off the coast of South America, only six minutes after the Anchorage quake.

The news station showed the shot of a rainbow near the Colonche mountains, one that vibrantly displayed deep cranberry, orange sherbet, striking yellow, Kentucky green, ocean blue, and a purple that could easily be confused for pink, before switching to downtown Manta in Ecuador, where street vendors were making last-minute sales, after a long day. It was a replay of a news clip that had been taken as vendors were celebrating the improvements around the center's city, giving them more space for booths, that they had anxiously filled with jewelry, straw purses, handwoven scarves, bright rayon sundresses, and an array of fresh fruit and vegetables that had been transported in by local farmers.

Paul watched as the video camera, one affixed to the top of a large tripod, suddenly began to shake, blurring the sea of different colored umbrellas, those hovered over individual stands in the busy downtown marketplace. The news reporter's hand can be seen reaching for the HD video camera, probably in a quick effort to steady it, and then in an effort to quickly attach it to his shoulder rig, just in time to shoot the uncensored graveyard of large umbrellas that had toppled to the dusty ground, amid pieces of yellow and red signage that once read *Ecuacolor,* now fragments of a plastic placard from a nearby corner building. Behind the cameraman, the sound of shattering glass and frightening screams could be heard. Clink. Ahhh. Pop.

Surprisingly, most of the buildings within the city stayed intact, something that Paul Wabel knew from his numerous reports. *I'm glad it wasn't much worse,* he thought, before turning his attention to a news story filmed earlier on Tarqui Beach, an area that had received the most damage, and one he could see had been demolished, as the news camera panned the corpses of newly constructed ship frames, which were now reduced to a panoramic pile of what looked like large toothpicks on the sandy beach.

It was a relief knowing the 7.6 quake off Ecuador hadn't caused more damage. He had stared at the damage report before taking his place on the sofa, one more time, allowing his tired eyes to read the number reported under the loss of life heading – *under ten*. He knew he shouldn't feel any responsibility for what had happened in Manta, Ecuador. *Earthquakes are a natural and unpreventable occurrence,* he told himself. Still, he wasn't totally relieved until he studied the up-to-date information from Manta's nearby volcano, the Guagua Pichincha, one that had shown up as having tremors in the last year, but had shown no activity during the last thirty days, not even a tremor. *Volcanoes don't cause earthquakes,* he reassured himself, before switching off the satellite T.V. and reaching for the satellite phone that was charging near his head, and one that was ringing to get his attention.

Always available. The thought stayed with him as he picked it up, knowing it would be O'Malley, his fat Irish fuck of a friend, that now lived in D.C.

"Paul, tell me one of your volcanoes within the Ring of Fire didn't start the shit off Anchorage or in Ecuador." Paul didn't bother to sit up, he simply stretched his free hand to the laminated map that covered one full side of his office, just above the back of the sofa. His pointer finger traced the horseshoe-shaped Ring of Fire that dripped down both sides of the Pacific, brushing the coast of Korea, Japan, and Australia, on one side, and touching the entire North America and South America coastlines on the other. *It is my baby, and those volcanoes are my children.* He thought about the years he had spent with them and took a reassuring deep breath before answering the whiny son-of-a-bitch.

"I triple checked everything Doug. Nothing was caused by one of *my* volcanoes." Then he became a little more defensive. "All of my babies are sleeping soundly." Deep breath. "And, goddammit, I've told you before, a fucking volcano doesn't create a fucking earthquake."

"You better watch your tone Paulie." He scoffed, before hanging up, without so much as a goodbye.

Paul Wabel didn't care. He didn't respect Doug O'Malley. First, because Doug always acted like his shit didn't stink. And, second, because Paul had learned through associates on the east coast that Doug was known for making constant racial slurs after having too much to drink, sometimes at parties in Washington D.C. and sometimes during business lunches. Paul recalled a recent colleague's phone comment during a conference call. *O'Malley said he was glad that Obama was replaced with a more acceptable skin tone.* It was hearsay, but from a very reliable and believable source, and the thought of hearing O'Malley say that disgusted Paul. *The proof was in that last fucking phone call.* Paul thought to himself. *He didn't even ask about Africa's quake, the most serious of the three.* Paul shook his head. *I guess to that piece of shit black lives don't matter.* Sickened by the thought, Paul settled back into a comfortable position on his leather sofa. *White supremacist house.* He smiled, after thinking about the nickname he used to describe Doug's favorite place to rub elbows, before continuing his private conversation in the silence of his office. *Well, O'Malley, the west coast is my house. Let them try finding someone else who has my experience with a Doctorate in Seismic Science and a Master's in Volcanology and Geological Hazards.* Stretching his arm toward his office wall, he rubbed his entire hand over the horseshoe-shaped pattern in bright red on the world map. *My babies.*

Realizing he was too much on the edge to sleep, Paul sat up, before making his way to his desk, where he flipped through a pile of paperwork on Manta. He knew it was a city with a population of almost 230,000. They had spent the last three years rebuilding, after a devastating quake in 2016, one that hit them with a magnitude of 7.8, and like that one, he imagined this one was caused by the Nazca and South American Plates, going at it like pit bulls in an underground fight club. *It's a matter of plate tectonics.* His thought came before laughing out loud, a reaction from stress, as his eyes traveled to another office wall, where he studied a sixty-inch by sixty-inch canvas print of Sleeping Lady. *No, Mom, a volcano can't wake her.* He smiled at the August twenty-first sky that was darkening outside his window, the same one that faced Sleeping Lady's darkened silhouette across Cook Inlet.

It had been a long tiring day. Three earthquakes and two tsunamis, all within a four hour period, and each one scrutinized right away by protest groups who wanted to blame earthquakes on fracking, others who wanted to blame earthquakes on volcanic activity in the area, and then of course, there was Doug O'Malley, an envious former classmate, at least in Paul Wabel's own opinion, whose job in Washington D.C. didn't turn out to be the diamond he thought it would be. He was under the constant microscope by the bureaucratic nightmare that surrounded him, and today, after the world experienced three major quakes and two life-taking tsunamis, he needed someone to blame. Paul's only saving grace was his skin tone.

Studying graphs and charts into the night, Paul worked quietly in his office. It was 10:30 p.m. The world outside his window had been shaken seven hours earlier. He knew friends and colleagues were with their families, sweeping up shattered glass, comforting small children, hugging their wives, and were sitting in a world where darkness, downed phone lines, and communication with the outside world was basically cut off, for at least five or six days he imagined.

Paul had everything he needed at his disposal – shatterproof glass, a mini-bar, a fridge, a sofa that had provided many a good night's sleep in the past, as it would again tonight, and a satellite phone system that Paul felt certain would last through more than an earthquake.

Still, Paul had no one to call. No family. His mother had died years ago, the last of his relatives, and he was too nerdy and too scientific to have a significant other, or at least he imagined.

Pulling an updated report off an incoming printer, he read the newest stats for Ecuador. Twelve people had been reported dead and hospitals had reported treating seventy-eight injured, mostly from falling debris. He placed it in a file with the volcanic activity reports for all the volcanoes in that area and wrote NOT CAUSED BY SEISMIC ACTIVITY on the documentation sheet stapled inside the front cover.

Then he printed out the most recent report for Anchorage. Seventeen people had been reported dead by local authorities and hospitals with earthquake-related injuries, again mostly from falling debris. He circled the number 112, the number currently being treated for injuries, hoping none of those were people he knew or small kids. The Pacific Ring of Fire was his family, and the volcanoes within were his babies. Every single one, all 452 volcanoes. He wrote NOT CAUSED BY SEISMIC ACTIVITY on the bright yellow sheet stapled just inside the Anchorage file, before placing it on top of the South America file, where they both would rest throughout the night while he stretched out on his office sofa.

There was no need for a file on Africa. It was not part of the Pacific Ring of Fire; although, Paul Wabel knew the area, and knew the volcanoes near the Ogo Mountain Range didn't cause the earthquake that shook Somalia. *Plate tectonics.* That was Paul's last thought before he shut his eyes.

CHAPTER NINE

ALASKA

The Haul Road, a nickname given to The James W. Dalton Highway by the locals, had slightly shifted since Enola's trip up, creating extra potholes, and a terrain that felt more challenging. *Why does the road appear bumpier?* It was a silent question she would have no way of knowing the answer to, but one that had been on her mind since morning, and since starting her second day descending the Dalton. She didn't know that tectonic plates, deep in the Pacific Ocean, whose job it was normally to move slowly and gently pass one another, had become locked in recent months, and even more recently, had struggled to break free, rocking the Aleut Islands and Anchorage. The 7.2 quake was enough to affect all of Alaska, even hundreds of miles away the ground had shifted, unnoticeable to most people, unless you're driving on a road like Dalton Highway, where every hole, dip, and drop-off suddenly appears exaggerated.

Enola eyed the open tundra. The fall colors were everywhere she looked. She tried to break the early morning silence with a witty one-liner for Miles.

"Look, even the buildings are dressed for fall." No response. She studied the dark brown portable, reminding her of a middle school classroom that Allie had spent math class in during sixth grade, one tucked behind Pine View Middle School in Land O'Lakes, Florida. This one was neatly placed beside a building, one colored a weathered Crayola yellow, and was a third its size. An Alaska West Express gas tanker was parked in the muddy lot. "Happy Valley," Enola announced, hoping Miles would at least sit up to have a look, before she passed the only sign of life she had seen since starting her early morning descent on the Dalton, a continuation of the evening before. No reaction.

Reaching Ice Cut, she slowed for a steep slope, making sure her Jeep didn't exceed twenty miles an hour and catch a bad pothole. The slower speed allowed her to focus on the sky. She watched a flock of whimbrels, birds she knew were migratory, make their way east. Her mind started to question the direction they were flying, but stopped when she came to a quick halt at the bottom of Ice Cut.

"Miles." It must have been the urgency he heard in her tone. He sat up immediately, watching the herd of caribou make their way from the west side of the Dalton to the east. There were at least fourteen. She had seen wildlife at a distance on her way up the Dalton, but not too close to the road, and most definitely not in the center of the road.

"Wow!" He paid attention to Enola's interjection, trying to determine if they were a threat. "Unbelievable." That was all she could say to her travel companion's inquisitive look.

Slowly, she continued, as she paid attention to every detail. Miles did too. His sleep time was over. As they approached

Gustafson Gulch, the Trans-Alaska Pipeline System, TAPS, rolled along beside them on the right, and without effort seemed to glide over Oil Spill Hill without showing any signs of exertion. Enola's awareness heightened when she saw a strobe light up ahead, on her passenger side. She came to a stop in the center of Dalton Highway, long enough to read the sign, then quickly continued. It read – IF STROBE IS FLASHING EVACUATE THE AREA. POSSIBLE HAZARDOUS ATMOSPHERE. Potholes did not slow her getaway. Her mind raced with worry, as her left hand worked quickly to make sure all windows were completely up, and her right made sure the AC was circulating inside air only.

"What the hell is going on?" She asked Miles. Even though he didn't answer, she could tell he was worried too. She saw a small workers' camp on the left, and hurried toward it, hoping someone could inform her about the strobe light. The entire camp had been evacuated. There wasn't a person in sight, and Enola didn't want to exit the Jeep in order to bang on the only door. *Forward.* She tried to smile, knowing that's what Dixie would say, so she drove. Hard. Even when the temperature dropped to twenty-nine degrees and blowing snow filled the twenty-second day of August air. Fall was over as she neared Oksrukuyik Creek, and the world turned white as she pulled to a stop near the Tea Lake Outfall, a place where she had minimal cell service on the way up, and a place where she had chatted with Allie. Now, nothing. *Maybe it's because of the snow.* She rationalized.

Enola didn't know that parts of the world were being schooled in plate tectonics. Rural parts of Alaska were just learning about yesterday's Aleut Island quake, and most had been unaware that the Juan De Fuca Plate and the Pacific Plate were long time competitors in a boxing match. News that would take even longer to spread, was the quake that had occurred just minutes later, as the Nazca and South American tectonic plates had brought parts of Ecuador to its knees. And news that most would never hear, at least in the remote areas of Alaska, had happened over 8000 miles away, a place where the Arabian Plate had thrown a Mike Tyson styled hook at the African Plate, deep in the Indian Ocean.

On the other hand, seismologists across the globe were completely aware, their evenings filled with information about the three quakes and the two tsunamis, and their mornings spent scrambling for answers. As a result, Paul Wabel hadn't gotten much sleep on his office sofa throughout the night; instead, he answered his satellite phone, which seemed to ring every thirty minutes or so.

"The three major earthquakes are not related." He announced over an emergency satellite phone conference call with Simon McKinney from The World Disaster Division in Washington, D.C., a man who answered directly to President Trump. "No, they have nothing to do with volcano activity." And before hanging up, "Yes, I'm sure, Mr. McKinney."

Enola continued driving with all the windows sealed tightly, not because of the extreme cold; although, that was a good enough reason by itself. She kept everything airtight to avoid breathing in whatever lurked outside her Jeep, and while continuing to drive another forty miles south, her mind replayed the flashing strobe light she had passed on the Dalton, replayed the flock of whimbrels flying east, and replayed the herd of caribou that had crossed in front of her several hours back. A vision that she couldn't see, and had no way of knowing, was that her Jeep was pointed in the direction of a major epicenter, and driving, something that normally relaxed her, was filling her with concern.

"Why haven't we passed any other vehicles?" She asked her driving partner. "Not one." She stated the fact, just in case he hadn't realized it.

Even though she had grown accustomed to rarely seeing a vehicle on Dalton Highway, at least based on her trip up, she knew seeing at least four or five truckers and maybe another two or three white work trucks, whose driver's job it was to service or complete maintenance on one of the access sites, was to be expected. Today there was no one, and the absence of other vehicles had started to worry her.

Wednesday, she had driven almost three hours after deboarding the Arctic Ocean Shuttle. And today, Thursday, she had driven nearly seven more hours. *Ten hours.* She thought. *I haven't seen one vehicle driving in either direction.* Again, she struggled to control her anxiety. *Holden Creek was a messy stretch of blowing snow.* She recalled privately. *TAPS was covered with frost and snow around Trevor Creek.* She was working to remember what she had passed since morning, in an effort to supply extra reassurance.

Atigun Pass was a nightmare. She thought about how many times she had considered pulling over since the day had begun. *Should I put on my tire chains?* She had questioned herself repeatedly.

"No." She corrected her attempt to rationalize out loud. "Something is wrong Miles." She made the announcement after making it down the last section of Atigun Pass, and after letting her knuckles loosen their grip on the steering wheel, just before she continued to talk to Miles. "There are semi-truck drivers that eat this road for breakfast." She recalled the show she used to watch about the Dalton Highway – *Ice Road Truckers.* The honest acceptance triggered every alarm in her mind. *Something is wrong.*

On her right she saw a sign – Chandalar Station. It was a Department of Transportation workstation. A metal gate extended across the dirt drive leading in, and before her mind considered parking and walking up, she gathered by the absence of vehicles, that the station was currently closed. *No one.* After her short thought, she considered letting her emotions take over, but then managed to regain strength as she caught a glimpse of the sun, placing itself in position, over the jagged rock on her right. She stared at it, watching a small bird hop from spruce to spruce in the foreground. Calculating the mileage, that she had gone since leaving Deadhorse on Wednesday evening, she knew she was thirty-five miles north of Coldfoot. She also knew there would be people there. It was a stop for everyone who traveled the Dalton. Laundry. Showers. A portable motel. The Truckers' Café. A small post office. *Forward.* She reminded herself, thinking of Dixie once again.

By time the sun had reached the earth's surface, Enola was only five miles from Coldfoot. She pulled over at Marion Creek to stretch her legs and to let Miles take a quick pee break, one that he seemed to rush through. Enola imagined it was the darkened shadow of a large moose drinking out of the creek bed that had rattled him.

"You can take a nice walk with me when we get to Coldfoot." It would be a celebration, one less than fifteen minutes down the road. Even Enola, who knew she was a good driver, had been pushed to her limit over the last ten hours on the Dalton. It had demanded her best, and had been a drive that could have easily tripped her up, one full of large potholes, rainy and snowy roads, and unexpected animal crossings.

As she pulled into Coldfoot, she noticed a semi-truck with the Carlile logo; it was parked with the driver's door ajar in front of The Truckers' Café. Enola smiled as she parked, noticing a pair of cowboy boots extending out the driver's side door. She looked twice, making sure it wasn't just a mirage in the darkened sky.

"An actual person." She happily announced to her co-pilot. Miles seemed happy too, until his paws hit the ground.

CHAPTER TEN

SIX MONTHS EARLIER

I sent Dixie a birthday card from Hcpe, New Mexico. Late. My timing slowed by a broken leaf spring on the camper, which I considered ignoring, until I noticed the 1963 vintage travel trailer sway and dip at every turn, fighting its loss of balance, and putting undue stress on the rear of my vehicle. It turned into a week layover, while the manager of a local service and installation shop tracked down an old leaf spring he knew wculd work.

Spending Valentine's Day in Texas wasn't my plan, but it turned out that way, after plunging south, an effort to avoid several winter storms. It was a failed attempt. An ice storm followed me, showing no mercy on my thirteen-foot camper, rocking her back and forth throughout the night in a paved parking lot in Victoria, commonly filled with RV-goers, except for that night. That night I wasn't accompanied by any other travelers or semi-trucks. I listened to the wind, as I reached for my cell phone in the one a.m. darkness, to check for storm warnings. *Strong winds and sleet.* I processed the information. *Twenty-four degrees.* I didn't know it had fallen that much; I only knew that Miles wasn't enough to keep me warm any longer. I repositioned myself underneath the blankets, pulling them over my head, encasing myself in a blanket-tomb with Miles. The lack of air made me warmer. That's when I heard the rain. Hard. I shut my eyes and moved my hand over Miles' back. The rattle of the camper vent upstaged my movement. It sounded like the vent was being ripped upward. Clink. Clink. Clink. It was a sound that lasted for hours. By three-thirty in the morning, I heard the rain hitting the camper floor. Dead-center. I struggled to think of an empty container, as I stood in the air that slapped my face with cold, before removing a half-used bag of dried dog food from a ten-gallon plastic bin, whose job now was to catch drop after drop. By five in the morning, I was reminded that if life wants to fuck with you, it will. Water had traveled the inside of the camper's ceiling down the path of a two-by-two and plummeted to my memory foam mattress. Miles was unaware; I was also unaware, until I sat up. All four blankets were soaked across the bottom third. My legs felt numb.

"I don't know what to do," I cried into the darkness, hoping Miles would tell me. He didn't. He looked to me for answers. That's when I realized I had to find more strength. "We've got this," I reassured him, as I reached for my knife and a roll of duct tape that I had in a small toolbox on the floor. Miles watched me work, his nose and eyes sticking out from one corner of the blankets, the part that had managed to stay dry. I smiled at his ability to take care of himself, as I stood in the center of the camper, wind rocking my thirteen-foot world back and forth, my bare feet keeping balance on a linoleum covered surface that matched the temperature outside – twenty-four. After cutting several strips of duct tape approximately five inches long, I worked quickly, rolling each one like a fat cigar,

and then tilting my head back enough to eye the drip line on the

cedar-lined ceiling, I stuck the tape barricades in the rainwater's

path, rerouting it to the center of the camper, where after dropping

straight down, most of it would be captured by the ten-gallon

receptacle that waited. Quickly, I crawled to the corner of the

mattress, making my way to the dry area with Miles, and covered

with the portion of blankets that hadn't been sacrificed to the rain

God. I allowed my back to lean into the corner. *A sitting position*

will have to do. I thought as I pulled my feet away from the wet area

on the futon.

Sleepily, I listened to the Texas wind howl, and even though

my eyes were closed, I did not sleep. Instead, I thought of Allie's

tenth-grade homecoming dance; she wore a cranberry-colored satin

dress, one which hugged her figure, its tiny spaghetti straps flirted

with her otherwise bare shoulders, and her shoulder-length auburn

hair bounced in long ringlets accenting her face: her eyebrows thin

and manicured, her brown eyes and full lips displayed naturally on

soft white skin that sported three or four small freckles, that only someone lucky enough to get so close would notice. She was beautiful. Fifteen. Then and now I wanted the same thing for her – happiness. I opened my eyes watching a steady flow of drops make their way into the large plastic container, before shutting them once again.

This time, I thought of Mitch. He was pounding boneless chicken breasts, between two sheets of parchment paper, using a silver mallet, thinning them out, so they could become a work of art, after spreading his carefully combined mixture of capers, mozzarella, pesto, diced tomatoes, black olives, salt, and pepper into each one, then meticulously rolling one at a time into perfect spirals, before baking. He never wanted to wait until the hot log-shaped rolls of juicy stuffed chicken cooled before cutting. Instead, he would risk getting burned, so his perfectly timed pasta could be served with the steaming one-inch pieces. It became our favorite Italian dish, *Mitch's Italian chicken spirals over pasta*, one that Allie and I would talk Mitch into cooking at least once a month.

I opened my Melantha blue eyes, after thinking of his. I watched the raindrops hit each barricade of rolled duct tape, wondering if Mitch would be proud of me, having carefully rolled

each one into a perfect spiral.

CHAPTER ELEVEN

SOMALIA

The small fishing village looked like a nuclear bomb had hit it. The seismograph recorded the Richter magnitude at 8.3. A series of rolling tsunami waves had washed ashore like large bowling balls, all of which seemed to hit the small village dead-center, nestled between Mogadishu and Jowhar, taking out the one pin first, and consecutively taking out every pin that followed. Strike.

Mitch waited until after Sahib woke from his nap inside the cave, waited until the young boy's left hand reached for the shiny abalone pendant that dangled from the green lanyard, waited while

the parentless boy's right hand wiped several tears, and waited until

rain clouds moved away from the mountain range, leaving the

ground wet but travelable, before making his way back to the lower

Shebelle.

"Hurry." He said to Sahib who was still studying the abalone

shell at the end of the lanyard, his fingers slowly caressing the shiny

shell, while his eyes imagined his mother's dark green eyes, the

same color that glowed most intensely from the exterior of the shell.

Remembering his mother, Sahib ran the tip of one finger along the

parallel lines within the concave structure and smiled at Mitch with

gratitude. For a moment, Mitch thought about his own family, and

wished he had something to remind himself of his mother and sister,

but worked quickly to shut his emotions off, by redirecting his

thoughts to the village he had left behind, the one he now felt

compelled to return to, even if it was to simply do an assessment of

the small community's fate. "We need to go Sahib." He said,

knowing that they could make the descent down the mountain faster than the time it took to come up, and knowing they could reach the small fishing village by late afternoon.

It was almost four p.m., nearly ten hours after the quake and tsunami had hit, before Mitch stood near the coastline, his eyes examining the home he had known for the last two-and-a-half years. He had planned to never leave, but now, standing there, he knew it was time. What few buildings had been constructed from cinderblock were no longer in existence. Bits of splintered lumber were scattered among individual cement blocks. There wasn't one structure intact. Instead, the people who remained sat displaced around small herds of goats, their only source of food. Others scurried to build domed-shaped houses, constructed from sticks and scraps of fabric, as fast as possible, partially out of shock, and partially because in another four hours the first nightfall since the quake would surround the torn village.

Mitch searched the crowd for familiar faces, as did Sahib, each hoping to recognize someone. Mitch looked for men he had worked with over the last two-and-a-half years: sheep and goat herders, fishermen, and crop growers. Sahib looked for his mother, just in case his eyes had deceived him about her fate. No one. The faces left were strangers in a sea of make-shift housing and wanderers whose eyes searched for anything valuable: an unbroken bowl, utensils, old water jugs, scattered pieces of clothing, a lone shoe, rope, or any type of scarf that could be used as protection from the elements. It was obvious that what had first attracted Mitch to the coast of the Indian Ocean was now gone.

It had been a coastline that welcomed him. Anyone willing to work hard would have his basic needs met. Not like the hamster wheel he had escaped, where his typical work schedule had been spending six weeks on and two weeks off a cargo ship, a routine which left him exhausted, and with a stack of bills that waited payment. He saw his opportunity, after the ship he had worked on for five months, without a break, docked in Somali, as directed by local authorities, after nearly being taken over by pirates. Operating a crane on deck, eighteen-hours every day in the hot sun, day in and day out, combined with slight PTSD from having pirates forcefully board the tanker he had been working on, made the small village just north of Mogadishu look like a pot of gold.

Mitch had watched the village he called home fight famine, watched people survive and grow, watched the unemployment rate decrease, watched people in the village fight back against terrorist groups that tried to take over trade at the coastline, and learned that survival was a possibility. Now, looking around, he knew the village would have to start over, but first there would be death, and plenty of it. *Death, disease, and loss of control to Al-Shabaab.* That was the thought that was most prevalent in Mitch's mind. Followed by, *most everyone will die.* He kept his thoughts to himself, before turning around and heading back toward the Ogo Highlands, and before speaking to Sahib, who was still at his side.

"Come with me if you want to survive." He said. "If you stay, you'll die."

Sahib didn't have to think long. He had no one. Mitch was his family now, at least he hoped. Quickly, he picked up pace, following him, away from the village, the only home he had ever known, and one that had taken the lives of his father and mother.

For a moment, he imagined Mitch would lead him back to the cave, but his new father figure avoided moving due west;

instead, his legs worked quickly toward the northwest direction of the highlands. Sahib fought to stay close to Mitch, his eyes on full alert. He was young, but not too young to recognize the dangers notorious for lurking in that area of the highlands. His biggest fear had always been the cheetahs, since seeing one run behind his village, when he was six years old. Now, two years later, he can still visualize the cheetah, moving faster than any boat he had ever seen crossing the Indian Ocean. He imagined that there were very few animals faster. He could still feel the fear race through his own body, as he recalled watching the cheetah clamp down on his family goat's jugular, ten feet in front of him. Blood shot everywhere, massive amounts, but what scared Sahib the most was the way the cheetah stopped, to stare right through him. For a moment, he imagined he was next, but was unable to move, his feet frozen in place, and his eyes unable to leave the goat's windpipe, that no longer hid inside the animal's body.

"Spotted cat." A quiver could be heard in his eight-year-old voice. Mitch sensed his fear, knowing they had just passed a large cheetah on their right.

"Cheetahs won't hurt us, Sahib." Mitch knew cheetahs would only attack a human in self-defense. "We won't bother him, and he won't bother us."

There was a part of Mitch that would rather face the unknown, then the poverty and disease he knew the outskirts of Mogadishu would be facing for years now. He had seen the dead bodies being piled as he walked toward the mountain range, away from the village, and was careful not to point the heap of human remains out to Sahib, knowing the boy's mother would probably be in the pile of discarded carcasses.

It was best to keep moving, before starvation set in, and before members of the Al-Shabaab started descending on the village that had been plundered by a natural disaster. He knew they wouldn't miss an opportunity to take the area over. The few villagers that had survived the earthquake and tsunami, would be killed. Mitch would rather be in the elevated terrain with places to hide, or as he formulated a plan in the back of his mind, places to pick them off, one at a time.

CHAPTER TWELVE

FIVE MONTHS EARLIER

Somewhere on the dirt road that ran along the Old and Lost River in

Louisiana, I remembered being seven years old and standing in front

of my second-grade class, giving an oral book report on Helen

Keller. I could see Dixie smiling in the back of the classroom, my

best friend since moving to Asheville from Detroit the year prior.

Even though I had no idea what it meant, I read one of Helen's

famous quotes in front of everyone in the class – "the best and most beautiful things in the world cannot be seen or touched, but just felt in the heart." Before I sat down, my teacher asked me what I thought the quote meant.

I don't know. I remembered saying.

I want you to figure it out someday. My teacher's words stayed inside me like an unsolved riddle. Until now. I flipped through my contacts, quickly calling Dixie's cell.

"Remember that Helen Keller quote that I told our second-grade class when we were kids?" I asked as soon as she answered her cell phone.

"I can barely remember what I had for breakfast." Dixie weakly laughed into the phone.

"The one where Helen says the most beautiful things can't be seen or touched." I paused trying to let her remember the rest of it.

"Only felt with the heart." She added.

"Yes." I smiled. "That one."

"Now I do." She said.

"I think I've finally figured it out," I announced.

"Nola," she laughed, although somewhat tiredly, "it only took you fifty years."

"I know." I laughed back, while studying Miles, his back legs extended, his front legs braced on the armrest, and his head stretched out the seven or eight-inch opening that I had made sure existed for him. He kept watch like a London warder. His Detroit butterscotch eyes traced every section of the tall seagrass that separated our slowly moving Jeep and camper from the Old and Lost River that ran through the bayou. He stayed on high-alert, ready to announce a hawk, snake, wild boar, beaver, otter, or possibly even an alligator.

"Miles does it all the time." I enlightened Dixie.

"What does he do?" She was ready for me to announce a breakthrough moment.

"Sis, he feels what he sees," I said, as I watched his crooked tail move rapidly from side-to-side. He had spotted a large black boar the size of a large dog. I slowed my tires to a complete stop while whispering to Dix, "Push the button on your phone that says *show me*." I said quietly, directing Dixie to accept my video chat.

I caught a glance of Dixie, sitting in a large leather chair, her body stretched into a full reclining position. *Treatment day.* I remembered after noticing a nurse in the cancer treatment center walk near her, long enough to eye the IV she had already inserted.

I tilted my cell phone in Miles' direction. A second boar revealed itself from the tall swamp grass. This one was brown, its hair appeared rigid, and when he turned his sight in our direction, it was clear he didn't feel threatened, as he was twice the size of the black boar. Miles watched the two of them disappear into the tall bayou seagrass that blew gently in the March air. I knew he was anxious to chase them.

"You don't want to go after them," Dix whispered into the phone, which I could hear over the speaker. "They don't play nice." She warned Miles.

He turned to face her voice. That's when I was able to show her. That's when my second-grade report about Helen Keller increased from a letter grade of B to an A.

"He didn't see the boars with eyes that functioned like a camera," I reported to Dixie. "He didn't process their existence through some hidden matrix of nerves and fibers," I added. "He would have known they were there even if he were blind. Every muscle in his body knew they existed. He saw them with his heart."

Dixie was quiet for a moment. I almost expected her to laugh, but was glad she didn't.

"That's the same way I see you Nola." The serious tone in her voice said she believed my theory. "Distance and sight never separate us." I felt her hug me from one cell tower to another. "You're always in front of me Nola."

"You're always in front of me too," I announced trying not to cry. I closed my eyes long enough to see her, sword in hand, fighting her metastasized monster.

"I love you Sis," she said, before her voice went sluggish. I looked at the date and time on my Jeep's clock. It was a Thursday. One o'clock in Asheville. Treatment day. My visual had been confirmed.

"I love you too Sis." Then I said it out loud. "Keep fighting."

I heard her mumble *okay* before the cell phone towers took separate corners to watch the fight Dixie had with her cancer cells.

Round 1: Chemotherapy drug Ipilimumab flows through Dixie's veins, causing her to sleep more than usual, have diarrhea that if not controlled could lead to dehydration, and severe skin rashes in locations on her body that she doesn't like to talk about. Round 2: Nivolumab fucks with Dixie over the next hour of her life, making sure she is exhausted and leaves her feeling like a ninety-year-old in a fifty-eight-year-old body. There is no round three. The crowd always goes home disappointed but keeps returning, each time with hope for better results, a process where vendors strike it rich selling souvenir t-shirts with the nicknames, Yervoy and Opdivo. The systematic and circular procedure keeps her fans coming back, their voices in a constant screaming rant: *Trick and destroy. Trick and destroy. Trick and destroy.* They were words I had chanted a million times in my head, and even now, I found myself saying the words over and over, until my eyes filled with tears, blurring my vision as I drove slowly along the Old and Lost River. I couldn't see Dixie with my eyes, but I could see her with my heart. Slowly, she took several steps toward me, before kneeling. Her body was poised, as her knees bent in a delicate curtsy, and as her dominate hand extended.

Horrified, I watched her surrender her sword.

CHAPTER THIRTEEN

OREGON

"Listen to my words. Hear them in your heart. Prophetic catastrophes have touched our globe. God has sent three major calamities to get your attention. The end is near." The Evangelist preacher's voice filled the corner of Alder and Burnside. His right hand held a portable megaphone and his left was raised to the northern sky above Portland. People came out of their houses and nearby businesses to listen. "Rapture is our destiny." He shouted into the bright purple megaphone. "It is not the end of the world. It is the beginning." Some people walked by, shaking their heads, others snickered, and still others, more than expected, stopped in their tracks, before dropping to their knees on the city sidewalk in prayer. Others began scurrying city blocks, to quickly relocate with loved ones, locking themselves in prayer behind closed doors with their children and spouses. Those in vehicles, slowed at the nearby traffic lights, purposely listening to Pastor Lewis Kitts, a highly respected evangelist in the Portland area. "The Bible tells us that the end of the world will be heralded by a series of major events, and I tell you that the three major earthquakes that occurred are part of God's plan."

Allie rolled up her passenger side window, still, her mind processed bits and pieces of the muffled dialogue that continued. *Disappear. Materialize in clouds.* Her eyes wished the traffic light had its own power system, as she studied the busy intersection, anything to allow them to proceed. Instead, Reese waited until two more vehicles cleared the intersection before proceeding through the area where colorless glass circles hung in the partially cloudy sky.

Chaos. It was the last word her mind processed as they distanced themselves from Pastor Kitts, and the only word she agreed with.

"We have to get away from here." Her voice seemed stressed. It wasn't the first sign of Portland's bizarre reaction to the recent natural disasters. She had noticed that the city seemed to be in a buzz about the three earthquakes and two tsunamis since they arrived late last night. Everyone was on edge. People were scrambling to fill vehicles with gas, purchase water at a rapid rate, one that made it appear as if it were flying off store shelves, and stock up on food that didn't have to be cooked. Just in case. Allie could feel the panic setting in around her, but she knew one thing; turning around and going back to Seaside was pointless. Word had spread quickly. No cell service. Most roads weren't usable. Hundreds of buildings and homes had been destroyed. Power remained out in the surrounding areas. Curfew was in effect. The National Guard had been called in to rescue people from rooftops. And, the part that made her fear for her own mother's safety – people were missing, and some had been suspected as having been swept out to sea. *Mom was north and inland from Anchorage, right?*

She questioned herself, meanwhile trying to reassure herself, as Reese followed the bumper to bumper traffic on I-5 North.

"We can't stay here, and we can't go back to the coast right now either." She processed her conclusion before continuing to speak. "I think the best thing to do is drive north." She swallowed. Hard. "Maybe by the time we reach Seattle, we will have heard from Mom."

"I'm sure she's okay." He knew Enola was somewhere on The Dalton Highway, away from the coast, and away from the nightmare that Anchorage was facing. *She probably felt aftershocks.* He imagined quietly. "She's inland."

"Just drive." Allie shortened her demand. Once again, she knew he wasn't being completely honest. She thought about the aftershocks. She had heard people talking about the repercussions at the rest area last night, some were discussing aftershocks as far south as Northern California. It was a distance that she knew extended just as far in the opposite direction, one that stretched to the top of Alaska. Panic filled every inch of the air up and down the Pacific Northwest Coast, and she was sure anxiety was especially in Alaska.

It showed in people's eyes, their movements, and especially their driving habits.

"Okay." Reese didn't give much of a response to Allie's last demand and nearly went off the road when Allie yelled a one-word response back at him.

"Stop." She shouted, noticing the car in front of them was coming to an abrupt halt, probably to avoid sitting underneath the overpass in traffic, a reaction that the driver probably had after thinking about possible aftershocks.

"That was a last-minute decision." Reese was referring to how hard the driver in front of him had slammed on his brakes, all to make sure the front end of his car wasn't shadowed by the overpass. Clear. "People think aftershocks can occur the day after." He shook his head, almost laughing at the way people seemed to panic.

"They can," Allie informed him. "They've been known to occur up to ten days after." The fact that she knew that made her worry about her mother even more. *What if she travels toward an area where roads and buildings are already weak?* The thoughts kept coming. *What about landslides? Mudslides?* Then, she asked the questions that bothered her the most out loud. "What if she makes it back to Anchorage and a larger quake occurs?" She wiped tears from her eyes. "What if the 7.2 that just hit Anchorage was a warning?"

Reese answered her by stepping on the gas, sending the Tahoe and camper under the overpass. Quickly.

His progress came to a stop just over an hour later, when they found themselves in traffic, backed up in both directions on Interstate 5, as far as both Allie and Reese could see. Shiloh was bouncing back and forth from window to window in the Tahoe like she knew something was wrong. Zeus had his head out the right-hand side, looking in the direction of Mount Saint Helens, his nose tilted upward like he smelled danger, and Yoda had made his way to Allie's lap in the front passenger seat, where she allowed him to stay, partially because she too sensed something was wrong, and partially because Serenity, had already been given front access, and was stretched out on the dashboard, under eerie skies. Reese and Allie both looked at Mount Saint Helens as they passed, taking in the grandiose volcano, almost expecting it to erupt, like it had done just eleven years earlier. Still they kept heading north, in the direction of Enola, who they imagined was at least another 2800 miles away. She knew her mother was out there somewhere, and she knew the best thing she could do was to keep moving north – closer to her mom.

"I've got to stop at the next exit and get gasoline," Reese spoke gently.

"Okay, I've got to pee anyhow." Allie knew she had to calm down. She didn't have a passport anyhow, and no way to get into Canada, so making their way to the top of Washington, up I-5, was the best they could do. Maybe somewhere along the line, she'd be able to reach her mother. *Cell towers will be working by the time Mom reaches Fairbanks.* Allie thought to herself, imagining her mother making her way down the mountainous and treacherous road from Deadhorse. *She probably doesn't even know about the earthquakes and tsunamis.* Her private thoughts stayed private, as her eyes were distracted by the long lines of patrons waiting for gasoline, a good ten to fifteen cars lined up at each pump.

Reese squeezed her hand. "It's going to be okay," he said.

"I know." She knew her mom would be taking precautions if she sensed danger, anywhere she was traveling; she just wanted to hear her voice and know she was heading back to the last state she called home.

"You go to the restroom," Reese suggested. "I'll walk the dogs and keep moving the car up in line."

"Okay," she kissed him. "I'll try to get more information."

Allie was gone thirty minutes, long enough to wait in the extra-long bathroom line, and long enough to ask a gas station employee about the earthquake in the Anchorage area. It wasn't the news she wanted. She walked quickly back to Reese, who had just let the third dog back in the Tahoe, and who was pulling the vehicle up another couple of spaces. Several cars were still in front of him, and there was more than enough time for Allie to reiterate all the information she had gathered inside.

"A trucker that stopped for gasoline this morning told the gas station employee that all of the roads northeast of Anchorage are now impassable. Lots of large cracks and sinkholes are popping up everywhere; not to mention that there will be a massive fuel shortage by the end of today, as in no fuel." Allie started to cry. "They're expecting large aftershocks and severe power outages." She felt helpless. "I don't know what we're supposed to do."

"We're going to stay together and figure this out." He was trying to calm her.

"A few people inside were talking about buildings that have collapsed and pipes that have snapped causing explosions all up and down the coastline."

"Your mom is not near any buildings Allie." He was pulling up in line, just as an employee came up to his driver's door.

"I'm sorry sir," the employee said. "We just ran out of fuel." And then, without further explanation, he turned away.

"When will you be getting more?" Reese called after him, but he had already made his way down the row of vehicles and was out of earshot.

"What do we do now?" Allie asked herself more than anyone else.

"They've got six or seven vehicles stuck here without gasoline." Reese started to explain. "More gas will come tomorrow."

He looked into her chocolate brown eyes. "We're not going to be stuck here forever." He said, then convincing himself, he thought about how the earthquake had occurred less than twenty-four hours ago. Correction – *three major earthquakes.* It was a thought that he found hard to process. *What was the likelihood?* He questioned himself privately, and for a moment, he considered buying into the possibility of the world ending. *What if?* It was a question he kept to himself, but one he wanted to discuss with Allie, another time. Now, she would find the subject ridiculous.

"What?" She asked him, after noticing that his thoughts were overflowing.

"Do you believe anything that the preacher with the megaphone said?" It was a close-ended question, and one he was certain she would simply answer with no.

"The world will never end," she said, but then added something that he never expected she'd say. "But it will never be the same as it was yesterday, even an hour ago." He looked at her, trying to analyze what she was saying.

"Do you think the three earthquakes will have that much of an effect on our world?"

"I do." She looked at Reese. "Everything changes. Relationships end. People die." She stopped abruptly before restarting. "And, daily events happen that impact people for the rest of their lives."

He wasn't sure where her mind was, and he was even more afraid to ask. *Was she referring to her relationship with her brother? Her father? Both? Was she thinking about her Aunt Dixie?*

Reese silently pulled away from the gas pumps, and off to the far corner of the lot without speaking.

It was home in their everchanging world.

CHAPTER FOURTEEN

FOUR MONTHS EARLIER

April showers came down in torrents as I neared Asheville,

prompting me to pull off at the first exit, so I could download the

hospice center address that Ryan had sent via text. *Hospice.* The

word still didn't sit well with me; it was for people that are dying.

Not Dixie. I had been talking to her every three or four days since

leaving Spokane, had been receiving updates on her treatments, had

been discussing side effects, and recently, had been hearing extra fight in her voice, until my meandering drive near the Old and Lost River. That's when I first noticed she was growing tired of fighting. Within twenty-four hours, Ryan called. *Rejecting. Progressing. Hospice.* The words didn't leave me as I made my way from Louisiana to North Carolina.

I arrived at the center by eleven a.m., after dropping my camper off in Ryan and Dixie's driveway. Room 118 waited for me. She laid her body facing the two large picture windows, with her eyes studying the eastern sky. The sparkle in her pale blue eyes had dimmed, and her face was in agony, but she had refused to take more pain medicine until after I got there. I gave her the longest hug I had ever given anyone. She had been through a lot over the last two years: her stage four cancer diagnosis, her mother's death, several new and different cancer treatments, and all the severe side effects that accompanied each new medication – yet, all she wanted was my company.

Dixie never had a hidden agenda. She was as real as they came. I had forgotten we were still hugging until Ryan Durant made his way toward me. Another hug, this one shorter, but just as real.

He had been, and still was, Dixie's husband for almost thirty-eight years.

Miles picked up on the fact that she wasn't feeling well, something he demonstrated in his cautious approach, carefully jumping on the end of her hospice bed, and planting himself near her legs. His eyes understood more than I cared to admit, as he placed his head near her hand and began licking. Alert enough to reciprocate, Dixie scratched the top of his head.

"Thanks Sis." She looked up at me after speaking, my childhood friend, giving me a smile that had saved me when leather belts and my black sheep status as a child crushed my spirit. I wished I could do the same for her now. My words came slow.

"Thank you for always loving me." I returned the appreciation she had just verbalized. "You're going to be okay." I wanted it to be true, but I knew better. I could tell by the way she had changed. Her body had taken on a frail existence, a shell of her former self, beat up by stage four cancer. She had put up one hell of a fight, and lost; although her spirit, a light found deep inside her blue eyes fought to say otherwise. The dimness that had taken over, still gave way to the light inside of her, the one that had shined on other people, lost souls like me, filling them with hope when they felt empty.

"I know you don't believe he's out there Enola." She managed to say between shallow breaths. "But he is, and I'll be with him soon." I knew she was referring to God. That was Dixie. Open-minded enough to respect and love me, a nonbeliever. I squeezed her hand.

"Well, when you see him, you better tell him he needs to start doing a better job taking care of this world," I spoke freely, with a touch of added humor. "I'm not happy with world disasters, terminal illnesses, or the cost of living." I heard her chuckle through sporadic gulps of air.

"I will Sis." She squeezed my hand, before letting the hospice nurse administer more morphine, which took her away from me for several hours, but I never left her side, and neither did Miles.

\#

I stayed in North Carolina until the first Friday in April. Each evening, I'd leave the John F. Keever Jr. Solace Center, and head to

Dixie's home, where a driveway lined with tall pines welcomed me to the three-bedroom, three-bath home with a finished basement, its massive outline filling the sky. Like a large dream-catcher, it had gathered memories and was working to keep the evil spirits out. The brick staircase had wrought iron railings leading up to a quiet world of wooden floors and leather furniture, neither of which had felt the bounce or laughter of a child in years, not since Allie and Mitch's once or twice a year visits, when I made my way to Asheville to see Dixie and those hardwood floors. I thought of Mitch as I climbed each stair, and thought of Allie as I noticed her high-school graduation photo in a frame I had sent for Christmas, five or six years back, perched on the fireplace mantel.

The hallway to the back guest-bedroom reminded me how badly I had wanted my second marriage to work. It was the same hallway I had walked down in 2000, wearing an off-white lacey dress, a tiny veil with matching pearls beaded into its headpiece, and ivory-colored pumps that had been coordinated with each. I had followed Allie's five-year-old movements as she tossed roses from the bedroom to the fireplace.

Mitch walked right beside me. His ten-year-old arm was locked in my then thirty-eight-year-old one. I could feel how proud he was of me, because I hadn't given up on being with someone, and because I was trying to make a better life for him and his sister.

I closed my eyes as I sat down a food and water bowl in the corner of the bedroom for Miles, closed them to the past while wishing Dixie was beside me now.

Placing my Jeep's keys beside a picture of Mitch on the walnut mirrored dresser, I studied his smile. Even at two years old, it was hesitantly crooked and unsure. The way he looked at the world when he was two was the same way he looked at it on the last day I had spent with him – guarded. In the photo, he was wearing a camo patterned long-sleeved shirt, a swirled mixture of dark blue and white, instead of the traditional concoction of dark and light greens. It matched his Melantha blue eyes, making them sparkle. I wished he was able to be part of my life now, a time when I needed him most. Dixie loved both Allie and Mitch, and had found peace and comfort after reading some of Mandi's texts and emails that she had received, and found regret in the empty space that lingered in her heart, one she had always saved for Mitch. I knew that emptiness firsthand and hated it more for Dix at the moment then I hated it for myself.

Being ghosted by the people you love is a different kind of pain. The pain is intensified because it is so avoidable; and the rejected only have one choice – keep going. Routine. It was a way to deal with the loss.

I watched Ryan bathe in routine every day. Each morning he would get up at five a.m., first to feed Josie and Kobie, then to have coffee while they did their doggie business outside, followed by a quick shower. His arms and legs moved out of routine, slipping on a shirt and stepping into pants, movements that fought the emotions he was feeling. I knew he loved Dix, my friend, my sister, and for that I loved him. He left by six each morning, arriving at the hospice center before any other visitors, savoring the private time, when he could hold Dixie's hand unsupervised. He needed those priceless moments; it was a treasured routine that I respected by purposely arriving two hours later, after feeding Miles and letting all three dogs out again.

Each day, my soul-stirring visit with Dixie was bittersweet, marred by her physical and mental changes: confusion, unable to stand, and inability to carry on a conversation for very long. That's when I started doing most of the talking, when I learned how to truly thank someone for fifty-one years of friendship, and when I hoped my presence each day made moments a little more tender. She was one of the strongest women I knew. *Maybe she didn't need me as much as I wanted her to.* I thought quietly to myself. *I know I'm the one that needs her.*

I watched the hospice nurse irrigate the intravenous port attached to Dixie's chest, watched as she flushed it with saline, then watched as she administered more morphine. *Please help my friend.* I prayed not knowing if there was a God, but hoping my willingness to believe, if only for one day, would magically cure Dixie.

"I don't ever remember feeling this awake," Dixie said, quoting actress Geena Davis from our favorite movie, Thelma and Louise. Trying to smile, I thought about how many times we had compared ourselves to Thelma and Louise. Dixie was Thelma: pretty, a little naïve, and kind. I was Louise, played by Susan

Sarandon: rough around the edges, didn't trust anyone, and not afraid to shoot.

"Well, we're not in the middle of nowhere, but we can see it from here." I quoted Louise. Dixie smiled, then squeezed my hand.

I remember her last words as I left that day. "Let's take off in that 1966 Thunderbird Nola." She pulled me close. "Keep going my gypsy friend, and take me with you, wherever you go."

"Okay, Dix," I said to my dying friend, amazed at the fact that she could recall the car that Thelma and Louise drove in the movie. "We'll be drinking margaritas by the sea, Mamacita." Her eyes fluttered just as I got out that last quote from Louise. Sleep had taken over. I kissed her on the forehead, and again on the cheek, before leaving, this time in the direction she wanted me to go. Forward.

CHAPTER FIFTEEN

DIXIE

Dixie died five days after I left her side. It was a reality that I tried to process, as my eyes squinted, to block the blinding sunrays that bounced off the Hungry Mother River in Marion, Virginia.

Standing at the water's edge, I thought about how Dixie and Molly Marley, a woman who had died beside the river over two hundred years ago, were so much alike. Both thought about the well-being of others, right up until their last breath, leaving love and compassion behind for those closest to them. Wiping the tears that managed to escape my nearly closed eyes, I thought about how Molly Marley had escaped with her small child, after being taken hostage by Indians, and how she survived as long as possible in the wilderness on berries and internal strength. Even then, in her last breath, she urged her child to keep going. Forward. It was a directive that saved the child's life. Found by another settlers' camp, the child was able to lead adults back to the site where Molly had taken her last breath, using words like *hungry* and *mother*, and leaving a legacy behind that Molly would always be a part of.

"I know, Sis," I said to the sky, hoping that's where she was, and imagining at the very least, she was a spirit flowing above me, like the Chiricahua Indians believed happened after death. I thought of the old man I had hugged near the graveyard in Las Cruces; he was someone I was destined to meet, just so I would know that Dixie and Molly were okay.

Studying the clouds in the sky, I noticed that the mass directly above my head was shaped like a large butterfly. Extending the fingertips of my right hand toward the otherwise blue sky, I tried to touch it, while wiping the steady pool of tears that blocked my vision, with my left.

"I know, Sis." My voice reflected off the Hungry Mother River's surface, as my chin pointed toward the Virginia sky, and my Melantha blues studied the silhouette that floated above me. "I'm supposed to keep going." My scientific mind reminded me that the clouds were moving as a result of the mild wind, a coincidence, nothing more, but my heart wanted to believe it was Dixie, an unproven theory that brought weakness to my knees. "I miss you," I said to the sky, as my face fought a round of sporadic convulsions, my last attempt to keep control, but something I was unable to do. Picking up the edge of my shirt, I collected a lifetime of tears for my friend, before looking up at the sky one last time. Empty. The butterfly was gone.

Under a clear blue sky, I wiggled through the Virginia Mountains, with my sticky face leading the way, and my raw thoughts dangling in front of me. Learning to grieve the loss of one more person in my life was hard, and grieving the loss of someone still alive, was even harder. Losing Dixie made me think of Mitch, and reopened a wound that had festered beneath my skin, since he had chosen to stay in Somalia, and since he had chosen to isolate himself. My mind flooded with thoughts of my lost son: his crouched position during t-ball at age six, his hands sorting through the mixture of sand and dirt at his feet, and the tips of his fingers picking up mole crickets, as their bodies wiggling for freedom, which he would always deny them, except during the two or three seconds it took to release each one, a taste of freedom, before it would be sentenced to death row under Mitch's toe cleat. Crunch.

Pulled back to the here and now, I answered my cell phone. It was Allie. She had received my text to call; her voice already knew it was about Dixie.

"I'm sorry Mom." She always put my feelings first, even though she had lost her godmother.

"The world feels smaller Allie." I was choking back tears, but staying focused on the road.

"I know Mom." She knew I was including the absence of Mitch, her brother. "We have a lot of people that don't care about us," she continued, "but Aunt Dixie did."

She made her point without much effort. Putting things in perspective always seemed to come easy to Allie.

"Our family tree is getting small," I commented, trying to stay in pain, and trying not to laugh.

"It has one fucking branch Mom." I couldn't hold back the giggle any longer when she said that.

"And you and I are the only two sitting on it," I announced, freely laughing.

"That's okay." She reassured me, then continued talking. Somewhere in her young words of wisdom, I realized she was right. *It is going to be okay.* I thought.

By evening, I made it to Woodstock, Virginia, where I parked my Jeep and camper in the middle of nowhere, on the side of a dirt road, the front of my vehicle facing large metal crossbars, painted in bright yellow paint, making them still visible as nightfall surrounded me. ROAD CLOSED. Knowing the Woodstock Tower could be reached by foot in another mile or so, I crawled under several blankets, where I waited for morning, as I snuggled close to Miles, who was already in sleep-mode.

Come first light, I would reach the top of the Woodstock Tower, after walking forty minutes up a small dirt path, littered with the last small patches of April snow and ice, and surrounded by the Shenandoah wilderness.

"We'll do it for Dixie," I said to Miles, before shutting my eyes.

The next morning, we did.

#

By the third week in April, Enola walked under a partly cloudy sky, passing white columns, the background for a group of protesters in front of the U.S. Capitol Building. One of the protesters, a woman around Enola's age, signaled her over, offering her a pamphlet about the environmental dangers of fracking. Enola stopped, long enough to glance down at the pamphlet, noticing words like *billions* and *hazards*.

"What is hydraulic fracturing?" Enola asked the woman who was armed with answers.

"Companies are using the procedure to extract gas and oil. It's pumping liquid into the earth to open fissures, so they can pull money out of the earth's soul." Enola noted the sarcasm in the woman's metaphor.

"Does it hurt the environment?" Enola asked, knowing the woman was anxious to tell her.

"Absolutely." She rattled off a list from memory. "It releases radon gas into the environment, polluting our air and contaminating our water, which causes cancer, heart problems, and asthma. She handed Enola a button. *Stop Fracking Around.* Enola laughed to herself.

"I guess I didn't realize." She pinned the button on the right-hand side of her fleece jacket.

"It can even trigger earthquakes by weakening rock layers." The woman reached down to pet Miles, who had been waiting patiently at the end of his leash.

"Thanks for the information." Being gently pulled away by Miles, she wondered how hydraulic fracturing could cause an earthquake, but imagined it wouldn't take much to trigger one in an area that was already susceptible.

Continuing to walk, Enola passed The Washington Monument, her neck slightly tilted backward, as she studied its goldish-yellow tip. Miles' eyes were more at ground level as he searched for a tree around the basin, placing Enola face-to-face with April cherry blossoms. Her blue eyes swam in a sea of pink and white, as a sense of power and strength flooded her emotions. She reached out to touch the blossoms that looked like cotton candy, examining their delicate five-petaled pattern, which reminded her of slightly deformed hearts. Their beauty made her think of Dixie. *Cancer.* She recalled the C-word listed in the pamphlet, as she and Miles made their way into the Thomas Jefferson Memorial, where Enola studied Jefferson's long colonial coat. *Did something in the environment cause Dixie's cancer?* She wondered, as she continuing walking in the direction of another memorial. This one Lincoln. He was sitting, his arms making full use of both armrests, his fingers relaxed on his right, and his left formed into a fist. Miles watched as Enola studied his body language. *Was he angry?* His face seemed full throughout the forehead and from cheek to cheek but dove into a sullen grin that was enhanced by a somewhat pointy and slightly bearded chin. *Was he aware even back in the 1860s that we were mistreating our environment?* She stared down at the pamphlet that was still in her hand, this time glancing at the back of it, reading about how Donald Trump signed an executive bill expanding drilling in Alaska, and wondering what Lincoln would think.

After having covered a lot of distance by walking, Enola decided to flag down a bicycle taxi. A well-built black man named Kevin helped Enola and Miles into the small carriage section, which was supported by two large wheels, and offered a cushioned bench. Miles snuggled beside her, but only for a few minutes. Once the bicycle-taxi starting moving, he sat up like a statue so he could get a good glance at the White House. Enola wondered if Trump was in there. Was *he* making decisions that would affect her life? Allie's life? Mitch's life? Or, more immediately, had *he* affected Dixie's life?

The sweet sound of a trumpet captured Enola's attention at the corner of Madison and Pennsylvania Avenue, where a man in a suede jacket and wool cap played *Penny Lane* by the Beatles, his body shaded underneath a saucer magnolia tree. *There beneath the blue suburban skies* started to play in Enola's head as Kevin pedaled

past him, and *there is a fireman with an hourglass.* She lost herself

in music until Kevin parked the bicycle taxi near her car and camper.

A vision of Dixie standing underneath the cranberry-colored saucer

magnolia tree stayed with her, as she traveled over the Chesapeake

Bay Bridge to the eastern shores of Maryland.

CHAPTER SIXTEEN

ALASKA

Friday's sky made Enola think of Stephen King, one of her favorite authors. An eerie setting surrounded her. This time it was a noisy flock of rusty blackbirds. She watched them fly alongside clouds that defiantly worked to pass them – *background for King's next novel.* The thought bounced in her head as her Jeep slowly maneuvered on the mixture of dirt and gravel, and as she passed a trio of skittish-looking Dall sheep on her left, their heads awkwardly lowered in persistent travel, as their spiraled brown horns seemed to beckon them forward. Enola pulled over for another bathroom stop, this one for both her and Miles; although, he hadn't seemed excited about walking outside since reaching Coldfoot the evening before.

Now, twenty-five miles south of there, a short distance that had taken them nearly two hours, at a location just past the South Fork Koyukuk River, where the greenery thickened, Enola's eyes searched for a safe spot to pull-off. Noticing a limited access pipeline right-of-way, Enola pulled her Jeep carefully onto the small patch of mud and grit, where a white pickup truck was parked. Empty. She imagined the person was working nearby, as she could see the pipeline's body wiggling in the distance, no more than a half of a football field away from her, like a giant silver snake.

Funny, it even sounds like a snake. The thought came to her, as she quickly pulled up then rezipped her jeans, after urinating behind a large poplar tree, one whose branches were filled with bright yellow leaves. After making her way to the other side of the tree, she noticed the slight hissing sound growing more powerful, and was almost able to pinpoint its location, a good twenty-five feet from her. Unaware that it was liquid escaping due to pressure, she walked closer, hoping to get a glance of the employee she felt certain was working in the area, another person to question about the conversation she had overheard at Coldfoot, after entering the almost vacant café last night, where two truckers were discussing a quake that had occurred three days back, near Anchorage. It was a conversation that held her attention while she ordered a hamburger and soda to go, but one she didn't feel like participating in. Just by listening, she gathered that it was the main reason why truckers weren't coming up through Fairbanks, and why she hadn't seen them doing their usual route up and down the Dalton. Not now.

As Enola relaxed in the far corner of the Coldfoot Camp parking lot, she processed bits and pieces of the conversation she had overheard. *Damaged roads.* She bit into the pillowy hamburger bun, allowing her front teeth to scissor off a piece of juicy ground round. *Deep ravines.* A large piece of Stupice tomato attempted to hide between her two front incisors but was quickly rejected by the tip of her tongue. *Electrical poles down.* Then, after taking another large bite. *Leaky pipes.* Satisfied, her hands worked to tear up the last fourth of her burger into extra small parts, before mixing it in the bowl of dry kibble that was being watched by the anxious dog at her feet. He knew his portion was coming, and he also knew that it would make the dry kibble more appealing, so he waited. *Timing is everything.* She hoped her assessment applied to the Dalton. It would continue to be a drive that required patience and extra caution, and one she knew she was capable of doing.

Standing near the pipeline now, she was disappointed that she didn't see a worker nearby, another chance to ask about road conditions, phone service, and the fate of Anchorage; although, the disappointment that filled the air around her quickly morphed into a strong familiar pungent odor, one that seemed to linger in her nasal cavity. *Rotten eggs.* She recognized the smell, one that reminded her of a childhood memory, a hot Saturday afternoon on Fourth of July weekend, one where she hid in the next-door neighbor's large chicken coop, an attempt to conceal herself from the only father she knew at the time – Dacey Fears. Enola could still see her eight-year-old self, sitting on scattered mounds of hay, between cages that held eggs, most of which hadn't been gathered since the day before, and many of which were rotting in Asheville's summer heat. It was a spot where Dacey never looked, mostly because of the rancid smell, and one where Enola often took cover, a spot where Dacey's leather belt couldn't find her. Looking down at Miles, she reacted to the familiar smell.

"Gross." She looked at him, wondering if his doggy nose had picked up the strong odor. Affirmation was immediate. She noticed his hotdog colored snout pointed in the direction of the powerful odor, the sides of it pulsating, after releasing large amounts of air, before sucking large amounts back in. The twitching motion of Miles' nose was the last thing Enola saw before an explosion knocked them both to the ground, where a thicket of shrubs offered a slight padding over an overwise rocky surface.

A canopy of bright yellow leaves separated Enola's face from the sun directly above her. Every muscle in her body was being held captive by the ground. She couldn't move her arms but sensed there was a bed of lichen underneath her fingertips. *Mushy. Spongy.* Her mind worked to process the texture. A series of words slowly followed in her thoughts. *Soft. Wet. Bologna.* Enola tried to smile, after realizing she wasn't dead. *Baloney.* She corrected her last thought, as her mind registered the texture of Miles' tongue, one that constantly licked her pinky finger, as he stretched on the ground beside her.

You okay? It was a question she was unable to ask out loud, not while her body fought to breathe. Instinctively, Miles must have sensed her concern, as his body moved several feet, before resettling close to her face.

Time seemed full of empty space, something Enola tried to fill-in by recalling events that had occurred since leaving Spokane. *Sumas border customs before crossing into Abbottsford.* She knew that was the area where she entered after leaving Washington state, and after visiting her daughter. *Allie.* She pictured her daughter's face, as her mind processed the last phone call they had shared, before boarding the Arctic Ocean Shuttle. She recalled her disappointment after discovering that Coldfoot hadn't had phone service since the earthquake. She had looked forward to talking to Allie all the way from Deadhorse. *The Dalton.* Her lips mouthed her current location but were unable to create sound. *Creamy coleslaw.* She felt the damp texture of mayonnaise and cabbage, as she parted her lips. *Golden fried chicken.* She knew she was thinking of Herbies Drive-In, a place she had stopped in Cache Creek, British Columbia, as she felt the crunchy texture of the crisp chicken skin inside her mouth. Keeping her head steady, she tried not to choke, after realizing that she was unable to raise either arm toward her face, an action she needed to complete to pull the chicken bone loose from her teeth's grip.

Enola tried to steady her hands, after sensing that they were wiggling like hooked fish at her side. As she lay, arms still, she imagined a large blonde grizzly rubbing its nose against her lethargic limb. She felt powerless. Her mind crunched numbers. *4200 miles.* It was the distance from Spokane to Prudhoe Bay. *4200.* She thought again.

Enola's thoughts stopped when her tongue discovered the fried chicken's true identity – tiny bits of gravel, which tasted nothing like the fried chicken she had devoured in Cache Creek. Her tongue worked to push out a mouthful of grass and small twigs, something she realized wasn't coleslaw, followed by dirt and tiny bits of rock.

Reality took hold, allowing her to process the soft touch that had explored every part of her lifeless body. *It's not a grizzly.* She corrected her thoughts. Her mind now understood it belonged to her faithful travel companion.

"Miles." This time his name escaped her, as she realized the severity of the explosion, and as she focused on his Detroit butterscotch eyes, a color that worked like smelling salts, arousing the deepest parts of her consciousness, and triggering missing memories. "Bobby Harb." She spoke his name next, even though he wasn't there. *He's dead.* She remembered. Still his name was enough to trick her body into moving.

Working her way into a sitting position, she allowed her vision to be level with the sun that had assumed the two-p.m. position, its sixty-degree angle a replica of the one she had watched for several hours, until it dipped into the Yukon River in Canada. Gaps of lost time became smaller, and details of Enola's life since leaving the lower forty-eight came back to her: sitting by the Swift River in Yukon; eating fish and chips at a mom and pop wooden diner, its entrance a dusty porch, in nearby Teslin; walking around the Takhini Valley salt flats; stopping to take a picture of Mount Hubbard, Canada's highest glacier peak; and walking barefoot on the shores of Destruction Bay, where she constantly stooped to pick up tiny green stones, some she felt certain were jade.

"I remember." She looked at Miles, his face waiting for her mind to catch up. "We traveled through British Columbia and the Yukon, just to get here." Her body moved slowly into a standing position, first on all fours, then to her knees, and finally, like a pink flamingo, she worked herself into a one-legged balance before administering both. She knew it had been a serious fall, one that she now knew had been caused by an explosion. Now, standing with her face toward the silver snake, she continued to address Miles who was faithfully standing near her, while she examined her extremities.

"We spent time in Tok, Glennallen, Mendeltna, Anchorage, Fairbanks, Denali, and …" She stopped rattling off places that she distinctly remembered spending time in, after her eyes studied the silver snake in front of her.

Flames. It was a delayed thought, one that seemed to take longer than usual to process. Paralyzed, she watched the mixture of carbon and hydrogen burn, as her mind evaluated the movement of the bright orange-red fire that danced in midair over the damaged section of the pipeline. Her feet wanted to run; but instead, she stayed planted, her eyes tantalized as the tips of the highest flames turned into pale yellow, with a subtle hint of lime green. There was a part of her that couldn't help but admire its beauty.

Miles beckoned her feet into action; Enola impulsively ran in the direction of the Jeep.

CHAPTER SEVENTEEN

THREE MONTHS EARLIER

"I feel like the song was talking about time running out Miles." I

waited for him to agree with me, but he didn't, at least not in words;

instead, he continued to pull me around Walden Pond in Concord.

The tall pines reflected off the pond's surface, reminding me of

Asheville and my childhood friend. Miles stopped, taking a long

moment to look at me, while he took a deep breath of Massachusetts air, which I immediately took as a sign that he agreed with me about the song *Penny Lane.* "It is about time running out," I announced.

The analysis made me think of Dixie, a forever piece of my past. With each step, I tried to convince myself that she wasn't gone. *Great people live on in nature.* I imagined.

Approaching a replica of the cabin Thoreau lived in for two years, I wondered what it would have been like to live alone in a cabin, surrounded by wilderness in 1845. I wanted to tell myself I could do it, after I had spent the morning shampooing and then rinsing my hair using bottled water, after I had brushed my teeth over a small trash can, after I had used aloe wipes to wash all my hidden areas, and after I had stepped into a fresh pair of blue cotton underwear and pulled on a crème colored bra, in forty-two degrees. I had managed. Finishing my attire with a long-sleeved gray flannel pull-over and a striped blue and white hoodie, which matched a pair of jeans that I slipped back on for a third day, I made a morning trip to McDonald's, where I had ordered a bacon, egg, and cheese biscuit with extra bacon. The early morning flashback made me laugh at myself, after fully comprehending that going to McDonald's wasn't an option for Thoreau. It was a privilege that Miles wouldn't have been as happy living without; he craved his share of the biscuit – several bites of egg and one strip of bacon.

I carried my thoughts about people living on in nature with me, as I walked the 1.5-mile path around Walden Pond, almost two hours with Miles, at a slow steady pace, stopping to pick up an occasional flat stone, as I tried to recall how to skip a rock, something I often did near the cabin in North Carolina as a child, and something I wanted to reenact. After making several failed attempts, I spotted a stone at my feet, which appeared flat; it was the perfect size and somewhat triangular in shape. Picking it up, I held it between my thumb and middle finger, in my right hand. Then, I assigned my index finger the job of increasing its spin, before lowering my body at an angle, my knees slightly bent, and quickly pulling my arm back, before releasing the stone in one motion. Watching it spin mid-air and bounce off the pond's surface, I counted with my eyes. One. Two. Three.

"Trifecta!" I excitedly announced to Miles, hoping he witnessed my three-bounce succession. He seemed to be staring at the pond's surface, where the stone had last rested, for a brief second, before sinking to its death. Tears ran down my face, as I thought about the stone's lonely decline to the bottom of the pond, just over 100 feet, a depth that had been measured by Thoreau, but one that had been declared as infinite by some people, according to my college professor, Dr. May.

I stood there, in Concord, Massachusetts, thinking about how most people needed to believe in infinity.

"What do you believe?" I questioned Miles. No answer. Then I remembered Thoreau's view, one that fascinated me when I read it in Dr. May's English Lit class. He didn't believe that the Earth should be less valued than heaven; he felt heaven was within us, within nature – right here. I thought about Thoreau's belief. To me it made sense. Thinking back, I recalled the lengthy class discussion we had about the two astral planes located on Earth. Some believed there was a place in the upper atmosphere where heaven was located, and some believed there was a place in the lower astral plane on Earth where hell was located. The conversation and constructive banter continued for hours, so much so that we had to leave the classroom and go to the refectory down the hallway. *Heaven and hell are places within each person. They are not actual places.* John Cumberland, a twenty-six-year-old classmate, was well-liked, his stature towering over everyone else, not only in height, but also in his position as the quarterback on UCF's football team. Polite silence took over the small group following his baritone announcement, most shaking their heads in disagreement. I sat there, speechless at first, not because I disagreed, but because someone finally said something that made sense.

Heaven is under our feet as well as over our heads. I still remember the look I got from most of the students in the group, after breaking the silence with Henry David Thoreau's quote. I could tell the disapproving faces were stuck in the cycle of childhood conditioning. As a child, I too had been conditioned to look up, had been taught that heaven was a place far above the clouds, and had been taught to fear the wraths of hell below my feet. Now, after peeling away the expectations, and after allowing myself to question and seek, I believed that heaven and hell were conditions not places, and that they were within each one of us. *Heaven is everywhere.* I not only remember saying that, but I can still feel John

Cumberland's smile staring through me.

It was a deep approving smile, accompanied by a stare that

examined every part of me, just like the gaze I was currently

shooting across the top of Walden Pond. The rock that had entered

the water had long disappeared, but the ripples remained. Minutes

passed, but I could still see tiny bubbles playing with the top of the

silver-coated blue surface. My mind rationalized that a mixture of

oxygen and carbon dioxide created the bubbles on Walden's surface,

but my heart wanted to believe it was communication from the spirit

world.

Somewhere between the two hypotheses, and only for a brief

moment, I saw Dixie.

CHAPTER EIGHTEEN

SOMALIA

"River horse," Sahib whispered, knowing the river he followed aside Mitch was the Shebelle, or as his father used to call it, the Tiger River, and also knowing it was home for reptiles, amphibians, and occasionally large mammals.

"It's huge." Mitch acknowledged the large mammal. Its eyes appeared to be black marbles, which stared in their direction as they neared, but didn't seem bothered, submerging and then reappearing every now and then, on stumpy legs in the murky water.

"Hippopotamus," Mitch followed up.

"Kiboko," Sahib added, sharing the name in Swahili. His

father would be proud.

They stopped long enough to catch their breath from

exhaustion and hunger while watching the hippo. He appeared to be

sweating blood in the muddy water. Mitch suspected it was the red

tint of the Shebelle River, knowing hippos don't sweat, but quickly

surmised it was more than the red water when he saw the spot

around the hippo's back leg darken and sensed the hippo was trying

to pull away unsuccessfully. *Croc,* he thought. He knew a crocodile

sometimes would attack a single hippo. He pulled his Smith and

Wesson knife from his still wet boot, after unlatching it, one-handed,

something he had become quite good at. Now, it was the only thing

he owned from his life in America, besides the clothes on his back,

after tossing his lucky lighter into the fire, during their sanctuary

inside the cave, and since giving the green lanyard, its surface

embedded with the letters N and Y, in equal spacing throughout the

mixture of silk and linen, to Sahib. It was something the young boy proudly wore around his neck, with the shiny piece of abalone dangling on his chest.

Looking down at the knife in his hand, he caught a glance of his own exterior: a blue button-down shirt, its texture a light denim, and a pair of Todd Shelton jeans, a pair he had picked up in East Rutherford, New Jersey. As he walked toward the river, he imagined his other clothing was now probably part of a fabric roof on someone's make-shift hut in the small village he had left behind.

"I guess I'll be getting all these clothes wet again." He said to Sahib, who stood frozen, with a long fearful list of *what-ifs* written across his face. The first one was for Mitch's safety, as he watched him swim out toward the hippo. His second fear was for himself, as he imagined being left alone, with no one, a thought that was followed by the fear of starvation, the fear of loneliness, and ultimately, the fear of death.

Waist-high in water, Mitch's first thought wasn't to save the hippo; instead, it was to kill the crocodile while it was distracted with its prey. Firmly gripping the five-inch double-edged dagger, he neared the occupied hippo, and without a moment's hesitation, he felt for the croc's head underwater, knowing his powerful jaws would still be locked around the hippo's leg. With his right hand, he penetrated the croc's brain by jabbing the knife in forcefully, at a spot just behind the eyes. Done. The croc went limp, releasing the hippo's leg, which allowed him to slowly move away from the spot where he almost met his demise. Badly injured, he made his way upstream, where Mitch knew the severely wounded hippo would become a target, his bloody leg an invitation for other predators.

"Hungry?" Mitch questioned Sahib while dragging the almost six-foot croc to shore, but he could tell by the boy's eager eyes that the answer was yes. They had been living on wild sorrel since leaving the small village, but both Mitch and Sahib had grown tired of its sour taste and were having severe hunger pains. Water hadn't been a problem; Sahib knew about angling leaves to catch rainwater, knew to sit the plastic bottle (the one he had found twenty miles back) in direct sun, to kill pathogens, and knew which edible plants contained liquid nourishment. What he didn't know was how to kill a croc, and he was still wide-eyed at Mitch's accomplishment.

"Yes," He answered. "But, how did you do that?" He formed English sentences fairly easily, at least simple ones.

"I used to live in Florida, many years ago." Mitch looked at Sahib, a distraction so that his mind would avoid recapturing who he used to be – someone's son, someone's brother, an American citizen, and someone who was living by society's rules. Now, he was a loner and preferred to stay that way, forgetting who he once was. "Crocs and gators have a soft spot directly behind their eyes." He paused, unable to take his thoughts away from Thomas Circle in Land O'Lakes, Florida, and for a moment picturing Allie and Enola. "I stabbed my knife into an area behind the croc's eye and punctured his brain." He smiled, watching Sahib's reaction.

"How do we cook him?" Sahib asked, excited to eat anything but plants.

Mitch was already using his knife to cut dry wood from the interior of a downed tree near the embankment, his mind too busy to answer. Sahib caught on and followed his lead, knowing they would need a fire pit, something he knew how to do, so he busied himself collecting rocks and forming a ring in a cleared spot under several trees for shade.

Mitch nodded in appreciation, after emptying the collection of dried leaves, wood shavings, and desiccated tinder that he had collected from the inside of the downed tree, near the rock ring Sahib had formed, freeing his hands.

"Bring me green bamboo, Sahib." He was settled in position, with his knife ready to quarter the bamboo into four long strips. Mitch chose the most flexible piece, before cutting notches for handles in each end. Quickly, he thinned out the second quarter strip of bamboo, cutting it in half, before tying one piece at a time to the pre-notched areas. Sahib thought it looked just like a jump rope that he had once seen a young girl in the village play with. Mitch formed a "t" directly on the ground, over a carefully architected display of tinder and dried leaves, using the last two quarter strips of bamboo. Sandwiching the fire thong underneath the top piece that his boot held firmly in place, he grabbed the handles, and worked his shoulders back and forth, pulling the bamboo thong first with one hand, and then with the other, in a rapid motion. He could feel the warmth on the bottom of his boot. His body responded by dropping him to his knees, so he could blow into the pile of warm tinder. Blow. Wind. Blow. Sahib smiled when he saw smoke and hugged Mitch when he saw the first spark. It was the first hug Mitch had received in nearly three years, the last one from his mother.

Tonight, they would fill their bellies with croc. Tomorrow, they would keep walking.

CHAPTER NINETEEN

TWO MONTHS EARLIER

Allie turned twenty-four in June. I drove to Seaside, Oregon to spend

two days with her, the first walking up and down Cannon Beach

with Shiloh, Zeus, Yoda and Miles, until the sky filled with orange

sherbet and dark huckleberry, a perfect backdrop for Haystack Rock.

It was a day I was glad we had alone, a chance to untangle emotions,

an opportunity to put our feelings out there, about Mitch, and about

Dixie.

Reese had taken a job doing concrete work: setting, pouring, and making sure cement foundations were cured, minus any pores and cracks. I admired his hard work, even though I knew, like myself, they were anxious to leave and get back on the road, putting work and routine on the back burner.

My second day in Seaside, a Saturday, a day off for Reese, the three us went to the local aquarium, where with childlike eyes we watched a large sea star, as it used its five arms to maneuver up the side of the glass tank, and hover over an unsuspecting snail. Without warning it covered the snail with its transparent stomach, then after emitting an enzyme, it liquified the snail, which conveniently turned the victim's own shell into a miniature sippy-cup, something that would soon be tossed aside – empty.

A part of me felt sorry for the snail; another part of me respected the suction-cupped sea creature, who used his instincts to survive. I took notice of the sea star's eyespots, one at the tip of each arm, and wondered if he knew he had performed in front of an audience.

The production prompted us to start a conversation about survival, which hung in the air as we made our way back to Allie and Reese's camping spot, where all four dogs and one cat anxiously waited. Everything from stockpiling food, having an emergency pack, and finding drinkable water filled the night air as dog walks were conducted and dinner was prepared and eaten.

"People need the basics, but they also need self-defense." Allie chimed in.

"What are the basics?" I asked, knowing the question sounded way too simple, but one I was anxious to hear their answers to.

"Food and water." Reese blurted out with confidence.

I shook my head up and down in agreeance.

"A place to live," Allie stated, then clarified. "Anywhere that serves as shelter."

Their answers couldn't be argued with. Everything made sense. My mind was processing the list of basics but quickly refocused on Allie's first statement. *Need self-defense.* I analyzed my situation before commenting. *Aging body. Not as strong as I used to be. No weapons.* They were thoughts that described my

situation even though I didn't want them to.

"I think I should buy a gun." I could hear my hesitation as I

made the announcement.

"You should," Reese said. "You're always traveling in the

middle of nowhere and hiking trails alone."

"I do have Miles though." I was trying to play devil's

advocate.

"Yes, and he's an excellent co-pilot, but Mom, you know as

well as I do, that …"

"He won't tackle a bad guy." I finished her thought for her.

"You should get one before you head to Alaska." Reese was

still trying to sell me on the idea. I had only been back in Spokane

for a few weeks, still had most of my stuff in the storage unit in

Airway Heights, had sold my camper for a couple hundred more

than I originally paid for it, and was still living life on short terms –

renting an unoccupied basement with a bed and small dining table

from a woman I had met the year prior, something temporary, extra grocery money for her, a place I never seemed to spend much time in, mostly using it to sleep, and a place I could leave at any time.

The next morning, I made my way back to my basement hideaway. Four hundred and thirty miles one way, each one worth seeing my daughter, and each one spent thinking about how life is too short to put down roots. *Now is not the time.* I thought the words but didn't have to convince myself. Even though I liked Spokane, I knew it couldn't hold me much longer. Maybe it was something I saw in Walden Pond, maybe it was accepting the fact that my youngest had just turned twenty-four, or maybe it was regretting the fact that my oldest had cut me out of his life almost three years ago. Whatever it was, it made me feel antsy. Seven more weeks. That would put me at the end of July. Time enough to get new tires on my Jeep, buy a gun, put a few more items in my storage unit, and order a futon for the back of my Jeep, since I wouldn't be taking a camper, not where I wanted to go.

"If we're going to do this, we're going to do it right." I looked at my co-pilot, who seemed to want further explanation. "No camper this time," I explained. "We're going on roads that a camper can't survive." I challenged his wagging tail. "We're going all the way." I knew that meant to the top of Alaska. I wanted to stick my foot in the Arctic Ocean. Having heard about Dalton Highway, an unpaved road known for its extreme conditions, huge potholes, poor visibility, and isolation, made me want to tackle it. I knew I wouldn't be alone. **Dixie would be with me every twist and turn.**

CHAPTER TWENTY

WASHINGTON STATE

Friday afternoon turned into Friday evening under the seventy-degree sky. Reese and Allie were still stranded in Castle Rock, still without gasoline, and still seemed to be part of the majority at the Shell Gas Station – high and dry. Reese, tired of waiting for the fuel truck, drained the gasoline from the generator, that they kept in the back of the Tahoe, hoping maybe it would get them another fifty miles, to a place where there was gasoline. Maybe. Allie was looking at him, looking at everyone around them that had made the parking lot their home, and quickly realized that life had changed. *It will never be the same.* Allie thought about the conversation she had yesterday with Reese, following their wait time at the intersection in Portland, where she had listened to the preacher with the megaphone use the word *rapture*. She thought about its meaning, one she had learned in her high school science class meant *seize by force*, after a student in class questioned Mrs. White about why the carnivorous dinosaurs were referred to as raptors. Thinking about how they struggled to survive even when food was difficult to find, Allie imagined herself adapting to that predatory lifestyle. Then it dawned on her. *We have to hunt and scavenge.* Gas had become a valuable commodity up and down the west coast, and grocery stores weren't opening in the area because of the electrical crash, one that could take another five or six days to fix.

"Maybe we should take matters into our own hands." She broke the tension.

Reese looked at her and quickly realized she was formulating a plan in her head. "What are you thinking?"

She knelt beside him, mimicking his position, butt on the curb, legs extended, and facing all three dogs who were stretched out under a nearby shade tree. "Shit is going to get real," she announced. "People are going to start fighting over gasoline." Her eyes were wide. "We need to stockpile," she continued, "on everything."

"Allie, it was an earthquake." He wanted to remain reasonable. "The Pacific Northwest has had them before." He looked at her. "The gas stations weren't prepared," he rationalized. "They'll restock, and life will go on as usual."

"It wasn't an earthquake. It was three major earthquakes, a fucking tsunami that annihilated Seaside, and another that slammed into Somalia." She looked at him. "I don't know if my mother is okay! I don't know if my brother is okay! And, I don't know if we'll have food in two days!" She knew her voice was becoming hysterical like her thoughts, which were trying to process the possibility of losing her brother and mother within the same time period. "We don't know how bad everything is, because power has been knocked out in every place we've been to, because we don't have phone service, no internet, and no way to find out what the hell is going on, except for what we've heard from truckers and station employees!" She wasn't giving him an opportunity to speak, at least not yet. "We need to hoard supplies." She lowered her voice. "No matter how we have to do it."

"Steal?" He flat out asked.

"Whatever means necessary," she whispered.

"Gas?" He wanted clarification.

"Gas, food, water, camping gear, bullets." She was making a mental list.

"Allie," he laughed, "we'll get arrested." He looked at her. "And, you're overreacting." And, after processing everything she had rattled off, "bullets?"

"No, I'm not overreacting." She was going to do it with or without him. "I'm going to get my mother." She looked around. There were at least forty cars stranded. People were standing everywhere waiting for power to come back on and waiting for fuel trucks to deliver as station employees said they would, but that was almost twenty-four hours ago. Still no power and still no fuel.

"And, where do you suggest we start?" Reese asked.

"I saw a construction company down the street." She recalled how many times she, her mother, and her brother, had tagged along with Dwight, her mother's attempt at a second marriage, to his construction job on a Saturday, long enough for him to fill the company truck with gasoline using the pump behind their office, and long enough to step inside the office trailer to grab cold soda from the work fridge. That was Florida, and that was fifteen years ago, but she imagined construction workers everywhere were set in their ways, and so it was worth a try. "Now is the time, while the power is still out, on foot, unnoticed, a simple stroll with the dogs."

They left the camper and Tahoe parked near the shade trees, windows open on the camper, giving Serenity free rein to run back and forth on the carpeted flooring. Then, they grabbed an empty duffel bag, and a large black plastic garbage bag with two empty gas cans tucked inside, before making their way on foot to Wayne's Construction, about a mile down the road, while it was still daylight, a time Allie thought would be less suspicious. No one seemed to pay attention, and those that did looked at the young couple and waved. *We're just taking the dogs on a stroll.* Reese convinced himself, as his thoughts continued. He imagined what they would find. *Locked doors. Nothing.*

They were thoughts that ended up being wrong. Allie had been right about the typical construction office, where they quickly scored four cans of Chef Boyardee Beefaroni, a twenty-eight ounce can of Keystone ground beef, a dozen packs of Ritz bits peanut butter crackers, a four-pack of Green River soda, nine single cans of Dr. Pepper, enough gas to fill their Tahoe and reserve gas containers, and a Walther P22 semiautomatic with eight bullets left in the magazine.

"This doesn't feel right Allie." Reese was speaking out of guilt. "Stealing, I mean."

"I wasn't planning on stealing," Allie answered, before digging deeply into her right-hand jean pocket and pulling out a wad of crumpled currency. She handed it to Reese. "Here, straighten and count this," she said, "and, quit worrying so much."

She pulled open a center desk drawer, taking out a pen and piece of paper that had **DWAYNE'S CONSTRUCTION** written in dark bold print across the top, while Reese uncrumpled the money in his hand. She scribbled out one sentence on the office-stationary before placing the short note in clear view on top of the owner's desk, and before taking the stack of organized bills from Reese's hand. Eleven ones, six fives, two tens, and one twenty.

"Eighty-one dollars is more than enough to cover the gas, food, and drink." She made the announcement, as her hand stacked it neatly beside the note before she walked toward the door. Reese followed.

Getting back on foot was no problem. It was leaving by vehicle that would prove difficult. They waited until the air cooled to fifty-eight degrees and the Friday night sky had succumbed to darkness, before prepping to leave, first by using the restrooms that the gas station employees had left unlocked, a courtesy and attempt to keep peace in the tiny parking lot, one that surrounded the Shell gas station, and one whose main entrance door had been locked up tight since yesterday evening, after gas was not delivered as expected, and after employees were encouraged to use the last of their gasoline to get home to their families. Since then, Reese had noticed people getting restless, some irritated that they had no access to snacks or drinks, others upset they were being held captive in the tiny lot, and over the last couple of hours complete strangers had been arguing with each other. At one point, Reese and Allie overheard a man whispering to his wife that they needed to take whatever they could get from other people. *We'll do it tonight.* Her reply stirred an uneasy feeling in the pit of Reese's stomach and renewed his faith in Allie's gut instincts.

It was just before midnight, when they quietly loaded all the animals in the Tahoe, after discreetly refilling the generator with gasoline and emptying the remainder of both gas cans into the Tahoe's gas tank. Reese got behind the wheel. Allie called shotgun, after rolling down the front passenger window and placing herself in position with the loaded gun on her lap.

"Just in case we need it." Allie made her point after noticing Reese glancing at the gun. "I'll toss it out the window if we get pulled over by anyone official." Her follow-up was based on the fact that she wasn't sure if the power outages and lack of phone service would place extra police on I-5 or eliminate their presence altogether.

"We have to get out of this parking lot without calling too much attention to ourselves." Reese didn't address the gun. His only concern was starting the car and clearing the parking lot without causing a riot.

"She's on your left, three vehicles down," Allie whispered in the dark, as she watched the woman pulling on car door handles, checking to see if any were unlocked. Reese sat motionless, watching her, as the hair on the back of his neck stood up. He gripped the wheel with his left hand, and started the Tahoe with his right, before hitting the gas and speeding by her. Close call. Her eyes watched him, as he maneuvered by her husband, after his attempt to block the exit failed, after jumping in front of the Tahoe. Another close call.

Both Reese and Allie, knew they had too much to lose – a camper full of food and drink, a generator full of gasoline, a small handgun, and each other. Still, Allie was focused on not missing an opportunity.

"Turn left." She was taking him back to Wayne's Construction, a quick return visit. He didn't ask why, as he made a left instead of a right. "Top off the Tahoe." She knew the gas they had emptied from the two gas cans wouldn't be enough to get them to the top of Washington State, and would only leave them stranded somewhere else without gasoline.

Reese winked at her before quickly filling the tank. Allie winked back, before making her way in the business' unlocked door. Picking up the pen that was still within reach, she wrote on the same note she had left hours earlier – *P.S. I owe you forty more dollars for gas.*

She thought about the line written just above her addition, as they peeled out, making their way to I-5 in the dark. *We'll return the gun after I get my mother.*

CHAPTER TWENTY-ONE

ONE MONTH EARLIER

July heat waves bounced off the Spokane River, as I walked Miles

along its edge. Stopping, he went to work at the base of an old pine,

pulling dirt with his forelegs and kicking dirt with his hind legs. His

tongue hung in excitement, then quickly retracted after noticing a

small chipmunk jump from branch to branch in an adjacent tree.

Click. Click. Click. He tapped his teeth rapidly and somewhat

forcefully, signaling his regret in being tethered, and to notify the

small rodent that the leash was the only thing saving him from a bloody fate. I pulled back, to spare the chipmunk, and to continue our walk along the river.

I had spent several days rearranging my storage unit, making a few routine trips to the thrift store to donate clothes and shoes that I had lost interest in, and organizing things I planned to take with me to Alaska: a sleeping bag, a futon mattress, several blankets, a mixture of summer and winter clothing, a one-burner propane cooking stove, a small saucepan, utensils, a food bin, a small ice chest, a flashlight, my hiking backpack, my cosmetic bag, my laptop computer, and my new Glock-48, 9mm, the latter would be shipped from a business in Washington State, a Federal Firearms Licensed dealer to an FFL dealer in Alaska, my way of not dealing with the large amount of paperwork and judging eyes at the Canadian border crossing.

My gut told me I would be leaving more behind than the contents of my storage unit; I would be leaving parts of myself that I would never see again. Spokane was my pit stop – a place where I felt comfortable refueling my thoughts. It was my Walden Pond, and it had changed me. It was the place where I came to terms with my adult son's choice to isolate himself. It was the place where I grieved Dixie's initial diagnosis. And, it was the place that had given me a new start. I had always known that I could live anywhere, but there was something addictive about the Pacific Northwest. My soul belonged around plateaus, mountains, and shorelines. I needed the assortment all in the same state.

Taking a seat on a wooden bench that overlooked tiny peaks of white water, a mixture of ripples within the Spokane River, I signaled Miles to jump up and sit beside me. His Detroit butterscotch eyes looked at me, reminding me that he too was a gift from Spokane. I smiled at him, thanking him for being my co-pilot on my previous journey and for being one I could trust on my next. His look said he was ready for adventure.

"Miles, we're going to Alaska," I spoke to his steady glance. "First, we'll visit Allie and Reese." He wagged his crooked tail when I said her name, noting his approval. "Just one or two nights," I added. Then thinking privately, as I looked out at the water – *a chance to talk and laugh with my daughter.*

On the twenty-ninth of July, a Monday, I pointed my Jeep toward the Pacific Ocean.

#

Spending two nights close to Allie was a bonus before starting my journey north – way north. She looked young for her life, one where she struggled day-to-day, and one where she existed in the moment, with no promises about the next day or even the next hour. I had to remind myself that it was an existence everyone faced – a cold uncertainty. Nonetheless, we made the most of those moments, first by taking the dogs to a riverbank, where they jumped in. Miles cautiously entered, but only ankle deep, while Zeus, Shiloh, and Yoda fought to keep their heads above the rapidly flowing current. Reese tossed a stick out for Zeus and Allie one for Shiloh. Yoda and Miles galloped in the water's edge like miniature horses, kicking up bits of the Oregon earth. It was near a camp spot where I had agreed to meet them, tucked just inside the north Oregon boundary, and a stone's throw from I-5, which was my exit strategy, but not until I had a chance to eat a palm-sized baked potato, corn on the cob, and a T-bone steak the first evening, and one of Allie's specialties – spicy sausage with homemade mashed potatoes – the next. Those moments that I so cherished were filled with making matching braided hemp bracelets, which each of us promised to wear until we saw each other again, and picking blackberries that grew wild along the river.

Leaving her on Wednesday, the last day in July, was hard. I wanted her to hide in my Jeep and come with me, but her life was with Reese, Zeus, Shiloh, Yoda, and Serenity, the black and white tuxedo cat who had spent the last two hours chasing a piece of leftover hemp rode from one end of their camper to the other. It didn't matter how slowly or quickly I said goodbye to Allie. There wasn't a method that would prevent tears from leaving either one of us, and the part that hurt the most, was realizing that there was no guarantee for spending time together in the future.

Moments aren't promised. It was something I reminded myself through tears that blurred the bright lights in Seattle's underground express tunnel, a destination I had made by noon, and something I reminded myself a second time, after dropping my Glock 9mm in Bellingham at a licensed dealer so that it could be shipped to Alaska, where it would wait for me to pick it up, and something I reminded myself a third time, after I was processed through the Sumas Border Patrol, had grabbed the two for seven dollar deal at a Burger King in Abbottsford, British Columbia, and had settled into a rest stop off 16 East. *Moments aren't promised.*

I stared at the hemp bracelet Allie had made me, while my presiding hand dug into the Burger King bag, and while my mind thought of the matching armlet that I had last seen on her wrist. I knew she valued our moments together as much as I did. It showed in the way she treated me: cards, notes, special dinners, laughter, touch, smiles, phone calls, text messages, glances, tears, and the sparkle that she had when she looked at me.

Before switching my thoughts to something other than my adult children, I thought of the raw absence that lingered inside my heart, and even though I tried to limit the time I gave myself to feel pain, I allowed myself to question Mitch's decision to cut me and his sister out of his life. *Had he never valued our moments together? Had he not noticed the way I looked at this artwork? Had he not felt my heartbeat as I held him close? Why wasn't he hurting for the millions of moments I had given him?* Hours had been spent talking on the phone during his long drives from Louisiana to Florida, after

working on a lift-boat in the Gulf of Mexico. Smiles had been

exchanged over dinners and across football fields. My hands had

pulled him in for a long hug following karate class. His friends had

camped over in a sea of snacks and television shows. Go-carts had

been purchased. Knees had been bandaged. Stories had been read.

Photos had been taken, and hours had been spent searching for his

favorite jeans and most desired game for his Nintendo Game Boy.

Now, nothing, and it was becoming increasingly clear, that only one

of us would care if there were never any of those *moments* again.

Miles watched as one of my hands pulled away from the

whopper it had been tearing up to put in his bowl, long enough to

wipe the puddle of tears that had pooled on both of my cheeks. After

mixing the torn pieces of ground beef and hamburger bun in his

kibble, I watched him devour it, before stretching out in the back of

my Jeep Cherokee, where I tucked my feet and legs under a couple

of blankets, before positioning my burger in my right hand, and

making sure my line of vision was unobstructed while I studied the

Abbottsford sky that had begun to darken. My left hand memorized the rhythm of Miles' heartbeat, as he settled into a sleeping position

beside my thigh. One. Two. One. Two. One. Two.

CHAPTER TWENTY-TWO

ALASKA

Every muscle in Enola May Starks' body ached as she made her way back toward the Jeep. Maintaining a gentle run, she kept her eyes forward, while a smorgasbord of red, orange, lime, and green flames shot from the silver snake's belly just behind her. For a moment, she imagined being chased down by a fire breathing dragon.

Fumbling for the Jeep's door, she prompted Miles to load, before hurrying behind the wheel, where she quickly dug in her jean pocket and retrieved keys with her left hand. Her right hand waited

to take control, each finger eager to turn the key, as her mind

nervously reviewed the different ignition positions – first position

would turn on the electrical components, like her radio and

headlights, followed by second position, where a momentary flash of

red lights would illuminate in front of her, indicating everything

from the oil to seatbelts. It was a two-step process she had grown

used to, and one that was momentarily delayed, after she noticed that

the braided hemp bracelet, the one that Allie had made her, was

missing from her wrist. *My matching bracelet must have fallen off*

during the explosion. It was a somber realization that she had to

restrain herself from reacting to. She wanted to exit the vehicle. Her

heart pleaded with her, as each rapid beat implored her to return to

the scene, demanding a full search of the ground where she had been

immobilized. *It's too dangerous.* Her logical side took over,

accepting the fact that the bracelet would have to be left behind. It

had been a pre-birthday gift, and one she badly needed now, just a

piece of Allie to help her to safety. *Gone.* It was a one-word thought

that saddened her, but one that she repaired after one reach. *My crystal selenite.* She remembered the velvet box it had come in, before reaching into her center console, scooping and then cupping the golden colored crystal.

The almost orange-colored crystal had been another birthday gift from Allie, one she had opened in Anchorage, while nestled in a corner booth at a coffee shop on Twenty-ninth Avenue. Now, Enola had it tightly gripped in her right hand. *Palm size.* She remembered her first thought after peeking inside the deep purple velvet box. *Perfect.* Drinking a trenta sized green iced tea, she had listened to Allie tell her about its powers.

"It's a healing crystal, Mom," Allie stated. "Most of them are white, but I wanted the rare one for you." She paused. "I bought it from a woman that lives in Brazil. We met her on the coast of Oregon." She laughed. "A nut-job on vacation." More detail followed. "She was doing some sort of gypsy spell on the crystal." Deep breath. "She talked to us for over an hour, holding our attention with stories about gypsies in her family." The next laugh came from a deep spot in Allie's belly but stopped when she couldn't pinpoint her mother's physical reaction over video chat.

"It's a beautiful gold-orange and sparkles more than the brightest and most vibrant sunset I've ever witnessed." Enola held the crystal close to her face, allowing it to soak up happy tears. She felt an energy immediately, causing her hand that held the crystal to clinch tighter, as she fought to overcorrect a slight tremble, one she didn't want Allie to notice, and one she felt certain was just an emotional reaction to the story Allie had shared about the woman.

"Of course, I wouldn't have talked her into selling it, without verifying the spell was at least good." Skepticism filled Allie's voice; nonetheless, she wasn't sure if her mother had taken the story to heart, and wanted to expound the spell in detail. "It will keep negative energy away from you." She announced proudly. "And, selenite even helps with muscle pain."

Now, bouncing down the Dalton, every muscle in her body aching, she held the Brazilian healing crystal tightly, as she thought about her birthday, just seventeen days ago. Her thoughts continued playing reruns.

"Fifty-eight-years-old," Allie announced, just in case Enola had forgotten. "How does it feel?" Allie seemed to hold her breath, waiting for her mother's answer, one that could predict her own fate.

"I feel like life is getting shorter, but it's also getting better." Enola thought about how much she meant that. Something happens with age. It had mellowed Enola. She didn't react as fast and tried to prioritize which situations even needed a reaction. *If it's not going to matter tomorrow, it doesn't matter today.* It was a wisdom that had helped Enola filter her emotions. Anger, sadness, and fear were spent frugally. Each breath seemed to be a little deeper, and every smile a little wider. "I'm happy."

"You should be Mom," Allie said, her gut hoping that more of her mother would rub off on her. Seldom was she able to let things go. Anger was a reaction she didn't try to rope in; she knew she had inherited that characteristic from her father, Rex Narducci, and she also knew it had cost her – emotionally, physically, and spiritually. Then Allie added, "Do you like it?"

"I absolutely love it." Enola's smile filled the 2500 miles between them.

The conversation played out in front of Enola as she put ten miles between the flames and her Jeep. All that was missing was Allie. She wished she could see her face now, as she brought her Jeep to a stop in the middle of the Dalton, before closing her Melantha blues, just momentarily, so she could recapture what she had seen during the video chat: Allie was sitting next to Reese, their bodies on a blanket just outside their camper door, their faces aimed at the Pacific Ocean, and Allie's skin soaking up the salt air. Enola knew from the brown sand and white-tipped waves that they were at Del Rey Beach State Recreational Site, a place where Shiloh, Zeus, and Yoda could run off-leash, while Serenity got most of Allie's attention.

Replaying the video chat in her mind, and holding the selenite crystal in her hand, helped Enola replenish her mental strength; however, physically she was still hurting. Grimacing, she slowly tilted forward, allowing the lower portion of her back to break away from the ergonomic shaped driver's seat, before slipping the golden selenite crystal against her lumbar region. It was an exercise that would require an open mind and a little faith, something she had never given to crystals, until the coffee shop, where she sat for an additional hour after her video chat with Allie, her right hand scrolling through Facebook, while her left held her new crystal. Every fifteen minutes, she altered the assigned duties to each hand. Left – scroll, right – crystal. Then, left – crystal, right – scroll. And finally, the last fifteen minutes, left – scroll, and right – crystal.

She never told Allie about the severe arthritis pain she had noticed since moving to the Pacific Northwest, and she was almost embarrassed to admit that a sixty-minute pseudoscientific session with her new selenite had lessened the aches and throbs in both hands, but it did, so now, she was giving the golden palm-stone another opportunity. *It could be psychological.* She rationalized. Realism sat in as she focused once again on driving, but was quickly dismissed as she bounced south on the Dalton, her back forcefully being shaken, an action that should have caused more pain. It didn't.

Instead, she seemed more alert as she quickly maneuvered past Gobblers' Knob, and into a world that resembled PlayStation's *Dangerous Driving* game. A fallen spruce stretched across most of the roadway, its trunk charred and blackened. For a moment, that was all Enola saw – one lifeless tree; then, her eyes processed both sides of the Dalton. A sea of spruce and poplar smoldered, leaving charred bodies in its wake. The fire must have been recent. She processed, then scanned both sides of mile 128 for any sign of live fire. None. Tears fell from Enola's eyes as her mind processed the damage nature and animals endure. She reached around her lower back for the healing crystal, holding it against her right cheek, while her left hand continued to pilot the graveled road. Elevation increased rapidly after Enola made her way over North Fork Bonanza Creek, a milestone that gave her rearview mirror an isolated view of the war zone she had driven through. Now, at the top of Connection Rock, she spotted a white pickup truck with an orange stripe, pulling out of a nearby access road. Finally, someone in a vehicle. *I have to tell him about the explosion,* she thought, before flashing her headlights on and off as he neared. He slowed with his driver's window down, but only long enough to hear Enola.

"There was an explosion about five miles back." She estimated. He shook his head in agreeance, his facial expression revealing that he already knew. Instead of replying, he activated the yellow and blue lights on top of his pickup. *You did everything you can do.* She soothed herself. *Keep driving.*

Her skin warmed in the sunny sky as she crossed over the Arctic Circle on the Dalton, leaving one world behind and entering another. Within minutes she began a steep climb up Beaver Slide. Looking over at her co-pilot, she smiled. He had already forgotten the dangers they had lived through. Curled up into a fetal position with his Detroit butterscotch eyes closed, the mixture of ginger and white hair absorbed the sunlight and forty-two-degree temperature. They hadn't seen over forty in days. Enola tucked the selenite close to her heart, thinking of Allie, and wishing she could hear her voice, while allowing her thoughts to wander, until a large pothole reminded her that she was still on the Dalton. As she neared Kanuti River, she knew she was close to her favorite spot on the Dalton

Highway – Finger Mountain. It would be the perfect place to camp for the evening. They both needed rest.

Miles woke, just as Enola parked next to a valley of Alpine Bearberry. The bright red sparkled under the late Friday sun. After clipping Miles to his leash, Enola placed the golden selenite crystal, one she was gaining faith in, back in the open center storage area, where it would be safe, while she took Miles on a quick walk.

Enola didn't notice how his ears stood upright, didn't notice how his body became rigid, and most certainly didn't notice the P-waves that traveled underneath the ground. The push-and-pull movement replicated her favorite toy as a child – Dr. Do-Little Push-Me Pull-Me stuffed llama – one that was abandoned in Detroit, before she was told to get in the U-Haul waiting outside. Allie replaced the toy years later, after searching eBay, and after locating the vintage 1967 Do-Little llama. Now, that childhood play was being reenacted underneath her feet. Miles' paws had taken on the job of tiny sensors, soaking up information, trying to decipher what felt like hunger pains, from the underground belly, a rumbling world of seismic activity.

CHAPTER TWENTY-THREE

SOMALIA

Mitch wanted to stay away from Kenya, so he purposely stayed to the right of the Shebelle River. Surviving on rainwater and pieces of smoked gator from the night before, they traveled near the embankment, as they constantly kept an eye out for any Al Shabaab members. Mitch knew he couldn't chance being seen by the terrorist group, doing so would only result in death. *Be ready to fight.* He kept telling himself, as he steadied his knife in front of him; all the while, he promised himself that he would carry through with any action necessary, even if it meant taking Sahib's life and his own. *It's not an option to be taken alive.* The radical thought of committing suicide would be a last resort, but one he preferred over being tortured and having his head sawed off, and it was something he wouldn't allow them to do to Sahib.

"No noise." He directed Sahib, who was sticking close with watchful eyes.

Sahib didn't answer, only signaled his understanding as they carefully traveled through an area where the young terrorist group had attacked others in the past, according to stories in the village. The anecdotes were a sobering reminder of their ability to turn villages into war-torn wastelands, like the one they were cautiously walking through.

"Cow," Sahib whispered, after noticing the four-legged animal standing in a small unattended corral in the battle-scarred village. There were no people in sight, but Mitch froze in place, long enough to spot several small cows camouflaged behind a patch of African boxwood, and long enough to decipher that care was something they received only once or twice a week, judging by the hay's brownish tinge and dirty feed bunks, and something he imagined was performed by members of a nearby militant group. He knew they were all over Kenya, and he imagined by now, they were all over the coast of Somalia.

"Stay close." He whispered back, as he cautiously moved further toward Ethiopia, slowing his thoughts about the village he and Sahib had left behind, and speeding up his pace. Hours of silence accompanied their rapid and decisive steps, as they maneuvered the long and dangerous pass; still, he imagined it wasn't as threatening as what was going on in the impoverished area he had abandoned. He envisioned villagers being rounded up like the cattle they had just passed, some being forced into work tasks, most being slaughtered, and others being held for ransom. *It's better to not have ties.* He fought his thought, for a brief moment, as he remembered his sister and mother, then quickly became more focused on the terrain in front of him: a lush lowland of wheat and corn stalks. Somehow, they had wandered into a nearly hidden Daasanach village, where small tribal huts, similar to teepees, balanced several feet off the ground, on carefully selected tree branches, that had been sized into twelve to fourteen-inch stilts.

Mitch knew they might not welcome newcomers, especially a white man, and had Sahib walk ten paces in front of him as they approached a man that was a tribal leader. His skin was a dark chocolate, like his eyes, and both were sunken and weathered from a lifetime of daily hardships. He had very little hair, except for what looked like desert scrub above and below his sun-scorched lips. His body wasn't familiar with overabundance and only received enough nourishment to survive.

"Hujambo," Sahib spoke in Swahili, hoping the elder would understand he was saying hello.

"Ashamaa." Neither Sahib nor Mitch understood the salutation but continued to slowly approach, assuming his greeting was friendly, something that was quickly verified when the man signaled his youngest daughter, Abeba, to approach with a basket of dried fish. Mitch could tell by the old man's eyes, that he was intrigued by a young boy traveling alone with a white man. Still, Mitch carefully held his left arm to his side, securely hiding his unsheathed knife, while extending his right hand in a forward

gesture. The tribal leader reciprocated. Shake. Then smiles.

Sahib mimicked Mitch's example and extended his arm to

the tribal leader, before smiling at the young girl who stood in his

line of sight, her hands still holding the wicker basket. She walked

up to him, the wicker vessel planted even with Sahib's eyes, which

were focused a few inches above the rim of the container she was

holding, and probably where they shouldn't be. He couldn't help but

notice the fullness of her exposed breasts. He reached for a piece of

fish, hoping it would soothe the hunger pain in his stomach, since

they had eaten the last of the dried gator nearly four hours ago, and

since they had walked for the last eight hours without much of a

break. His hand tingled as he realized how close it came to Abeba's

chest.

"Thank-you," he said, wondering if she understood, but felt

she had after she reciprocated with a slight smile and dark flirting

eyes.

Her father signaled her back to the center of the village, with

instructions that followed her. Sahib suddenly recognized the language he was speaking – Oromo – after hearing the word *shiroo*, which he knew meant corn. From a distance, Sahib watched Abeba grab another basket, this one for corn, and disappear off into the maze crops which towered over her head.

Following Mitch and the tribal leader, he walked toward the center of the village, smiling at women's faces that were much older than that of his mother's, the latter a visual that he kept close to his heart. He noticed one of the women draining blood from a small cow into an old mug, just enough without causing the cow any harm, and without wasting any time after the collection, she approached the tribal leader, who took the mug in hand and drank down a large swig of blood, before smiling with slightly tinted teeth.

"Cadmar." The man said pointing to himself, a gesture which Mitch understood as his name.

"Mitch." He announced. Then pointed to the young boy who had become his right arm. "Sahib." The old man smiled.

"Maqa?" Cadmar asked. Sahib nodded his head up and down, after recognizing the Oromo word – Maqa – which he knew meant name.

Sahib thought of his own father, remembering their after-dinner routine: practicing Oromo every Monday and Tuesday evening and practicing English every Thursday and Friday evening. Wednesdays, his father always worked too late, and Saturdays and Sundays were reserved for being a boy according to his father. Sahib never practiced Swahili with his dad; that was his mother's language since birth, and one he would always speak with her. Now, Sahib was realizing how lucky he had been, having parents that cared about him and that educated him.

"Si argun naaf gammachudha." Sahib wanted to show off a phrase his father had taught him. Cadmar stopped in his tracks, turning to Sahib, and smiled an extra big smile.

"Nice to meet you too," Cadmar responded in English. Sahib wasn't the only one who knew bits and pieces of another language.

Mitch suddenly felt he had found his new home.

CHAPTER TWENTY-FOUR

ALASKA

For Enola, home was anywhere she happened to be. She had felt that way standing in the middle of Denali National Park, her back to the sun, and her face to the wind. It was a week after turning fifty-eight. She imagined it was the process of turning another year older that made her see how temporary life was, more so than she had felt just four months earlier. Of course, a lot had happened in those four months. But two things gnawed at her. First, she had lost Dixie, something she found very hard to accept, and something she never imagined happening. And, second, she had proven her abusive father figure, Dacey Fears, correct. It was something she had always known would happen, but something she wished he hadn't of predicted. *You've got a gypsy soul Enola May.*

She could still hear him say it, at the moment, and eleven days ago, as she took a deep breath of the Kantishna Mountain air in Denali National Park, where a sign reading – END OF THE ROAD MILE 92.5 – stood before her. *It doesn't matter that Dacey Fears knew that about me.* She reminded herself, after stopping long enough to snap a photo of the sign, and before picking a small handful of wild blueberries on a nearby vine. She stuffed them into her mouth, while Miles watched, his eyes wondering what he had missed.

"Here." She cupped one in her left hand for Miles. "Try this." Her voice was level with his eyes, as she bent over, holding her hand steady for the incoming sniff test. He backed away. "Seriously Miles." She stated her question, all the while wondering how he could turn down the fresh sweet taste. Enola grabbed a few more off another bush, tossing one berry in her mouth at a time, a chaser for each thought that consumed her since leaving Spokane. *Dixie's God let her die.* Berry. *Mitch has forgotten me.* Berry. *There's no such thing as a soulmate.* Berry. She looked at the last berry that rolled in the palm of her hand while searching her mind for something positive that she believed strongly in. *Allie is tenacious and strong-willed.* Berry.

Her right hand was uninhabited, but even though it was empty she could see where the berries had been. Purple residue remained. *I'll wash it off later.* She reminded herself. *For now, it's part of me.* She wondered if nature perpetually resides within a human body, and she wondered if a human body is everlasting in nature.

It was a theory about afterlife that she analyzed as she drove over Dall Creek, braking from her bumpy speed of thirty mph to a crawl of ten mph, when she spotted a mother moose making its way from the right side of Dalton to the left. Closely following, a baby moose, not much larger than Allie and Reese's Zeus, maintained a stride that kept it alongside its mother. It was a sight that brought

Enola to a full stop. Miraculous. First, to see a calf, and second, to witness the bond between mother and child. Enola remained silent, keeping comments that she would normally share with her co-pilot to herself. The welcomed silence stayed with her until Fort Hamlin Hills Creek, where she finally inched her driver's window down, taking in the air that had dropped to thirty-four degrees. The clouds overhead made the day seem colder, and almost hid the pipeline that wiggled alongside Enola's vehicle on the right. Her first word in hours came out as a question.

"Hungry?" She asked Miles. Time had gotten away from her as she drove. Hours had passed since leaving Finger Mountain that morning, and the time of day that would normally be considered lunch, a nosh-up, was dwindling. Enola recalled how she had passed the Yukon Camp on the way up, and had seen a sign for food, but didn't bother stopping. Now, things were different. The close calls that she had managed to live through since Wednesday, while making her way back down the Dalton, had intensified her appetite. Soup wouldn't be enough to get through the day. Miles wagged his tail as they pulled off the Dalton and onto a patch of bumpy gravel.

"Me too." She answered his gesture. "Stay here." She exited the car on her announcement. "I'll see if anyone's inside."

Fifteen minutes later, Enola returned with an egg, bacon, and cheese sandwich, one that turned out to be the best *linner* sandwich of her life, an adjective she reserved for meals she ate that were a combination of lunch and dinner. The cook inside had piled five strips of bacon on the perfectly done wheat toast, topped it with an egg that was cooked through, so that the yolk wouldn't run down Enola's arm while she was driving, and added cheese, which had been melted perfectly. Miles was happy to see the extra bacon. Not only did he score a portion of the egg, mixed in his dried kibble, but Enola took the time to tear up two full slices of bacon into tiny bits.

"Slow down, silly." She smirked at him, then realized she was doing the same thing. Within minutes all traces of the Yukon River Noodle House Café were gone. Miles curled up, leaning his head on Enola's right arm that had made its way to his side of the vehicle. She left it there, allowing it to serve as a pillow for her furry friend.

Driving slowly on the Dalton, she thought of Allie, wondering if she had heard about the Alaskan quake, and unaware she had nearly become a victim in its aftermath. Enola watched the skyline as the Jeep crawled along the gravel road. The sound reminded her of Los Banos, California. She listened as her tires ground tiny bits of rock, a sound that somehow comforted her. Miles rolled over, releasing Enola's arm, as he thrust all four paws into the air. Uninhibited, he relaxed each limb, while his butterscotch eyes remained hidden by eyelids that fluttered. Enola glanced over long enough to study his rapid eye movement. *Unguarded.* She assessed his posture, while trying to remember the last time she had fallen into such a paradoxical sleep. She imagined people her age seldom experienced REM, and as she slowly maneuvered the Dalton, she tried to come up with a theory that explained her typical sleep patterns. *Perhaps it's never feeling like I'm enough.* Her thought deepened and expanded into several thoughts. *I wasn't enough for my mother. I wasn't enough for my half-sister. I wasn't enough for Rex. I wasn't enough for Mitch.*

Rounding the last corner, before her thoughts switched to finding a camping spot, Enola caught a glimpse of herself in her rearview mirror. Behind her she could see a long stretch of the Dalton – a reflection of where she had been. *I can't do this anymore.* She whispered to her own blue eyes. *I can't let another human being make me feel like I'm not good enough.* She slowly pulled off the road when she found an area where she could stare at the Dalton in both directions. *The behavior of other people is not a reflection of me.* She announced to the woman in the mirror. *I was a good daughter, a good sister, a good wife, and a good parent.*

That night, under a sky full of stars, Enola slept – hard. Her blue eyes darted back and forth under eyelids that had experienced a lifetime of roles, while her body found comfort in the mountain air.

CHAPTER TWENTY-FIVE

WASHINGTON STATE

They had left the Shell gas station, right at midnight, after everyone

in the parking lot appeared to be sleeping, except for a woman who

was casing unattended cars and campers; she was the same woman

Reese had overheard talking with her husband hours earlier, the

same husband who had attempted to stop Reese and Allie by

jumping in front of their Tahoe as they left. Unscathed, they made

their way out to the main road, where Allie prompted Reese to stop by Dwayne's Construction, just one more time, to fill their tank with gas.

Even though living like gypsies often described their lifestyle, stealing wasn't in their blood, nor was living at the expense of others. But under the current circumstances, Allie knew survival would come at a price, and figuring out when to separate survival from morality would depend on the people involved. She had made the decision to leave money and a note at Dwayne's Construction, had pledged additional compensation for gas, and had vowed to return the owner's firearm. Both were promises she would keep when the time was right.

Now wasn't the time, so without further delay, and in the thick of night, they made their way up I-5 North toward Bellingham, the same route Enola had taken to leave, and one Allie felt her mother might travel back. It was a five-hour trip to Bellingham. Reese drove most of it with his headlights off. Allie rode shotgun, her hand on the P22 in her lap. Ready just in case. They passed parked cars on the side of the road, most abandoned, and out of fuel, but a few had *sleepers*, at least that's what Allie called them. She knew at any time a sleeper could forcefully try and pull them over to get food, fuel, or simply take everything and leave them stranded with three dogs and a cat. She even played out a worse ending in her mind but kept it to herself.

"We've gone 175 miles," Reese whispered in Allie's direction, his voice accommodating the unknown dangers lurking outside.

"That puts us about twenty-five miles out." Allie calculated. "I know my mom took 542 East." She recalled, almost able to hear her mother's voice. "Mom, stopped at Panda Express, as soon as she got off I-5." Allie's memory was vivid, even though it had been almost thirty days since that conversation, one where her mother had happily announced that she was only twenty-two miles from the Canadian border. "We'll find someplace safe to camp in that area."

"Okay." Reese knew Allie wouldn't take no for an answer. They'd have to lay low. Fortunately, the graveyard of abandoned vehicles worked in their favor. As long as they kept lights off, they wouldn't call much attention to themselves in a plaza surrounded by other vehicles.

It was just after 5 a.m. when Allie and Reese parked in front of the Panda Express. Daylight was quickly approaching, and Reese was anxious to get parked and settled, his mindset on grabbing six or seven hours of sleep, before making a late Saturday lunch. *Maybe the can of Keystone ground beef over rice.* He imagined the taste of consuming a large hot bowl of rice and beef.

"Squalicum High School is two miles down the road." Allie eyed the pink sign taped near the front door, making out the words: *high school, 2 miles, Saturday, August twenty-fourth, first car wash of the school year*, and an arrow pointing east. "The car wash is canceled because of the quake, I'm certain." The fuel shortage, cell tower outages, and electrical grid problems had literally stopped life up and down I-5 and the surrounding areas. She knew a car wash wasn't going to be happening – not while the PNW was at a stand-still.

They parked behind Squalicum High by 5:30 in the morning, where they quickly let the dogs out to do their business, then locked up the Tahoe, before making their way into the camper. Reese didn't want to run the generator, not yet, not until they figured out who was around them. Instead, they kept the loaded gun within grabbing distance, while they settled in to sleep mode inside.

Even after waking, nearly seven hours later, Reese suggested they use the propane stove, instead of the generator, which he suspected would notify anyone in the vicinity that they were functional, information he didn't want to share. The small propane stove would work just fine to heat the can of ground-beef they had taken from Dwayne's Construction and an extra-large serving of white rice that Allie had stockpiled, after their last shopping trip at Fred Meyer in Seaside.

Allie had charged her phone in the vehicle, so she'd have a full battery, just in case cell coverage was restored, and just in case her mother was able to get through. Nothing. Doing what they could, they ate white rice smothered in ground beef, fed the dogs each their own bowl of Purina One with a little rice mixed in, fed Serenity her usual – Meow Mix flavored in turkey and giblet sauce – and would occasionally lift a window shade, long enough to see if anyone was walking in the school parking lot. No one. Not even a janitor. Whatcom County School District had been closed since

Wednesday's earthquake, and would remain that way, at least through the weekend.

Darkness and conversation filled the small camper Saturday evening behind Squalicum High.

"How bad do you think Anchorage suffered?" Allie asked Reese in the dark.

"I'm sure they have a lot of downed electrical poles, shattered windows, building damage, and fucked up roads."

"What about Seaside?" She asked.

"The tsunami probably did more damage than the quake." He whispered in the dark. "Flooding, loss of life, severe road damage." He pictured Seaside in his mind. "I bet you the boat dock where we sat and watched harbor seals last week is gone." He kept talking through her silence. "Tsunamis are like bowling balls." It was after his last statement that he quieted, listening to Allie's breathing, and wondering if his words had caused her to worry about her brother. He had forgotten that Somalia was hit by the strongest quake of the three, and that it was slammed by a major tsunami, wiping out most of what had managed to survive the quake.

"Do you think my brother is dead?" She asked the question through choked emotion.

"No Allie," Reese answered. "He's too stubborn to die." It was an attempt to make her laugh, but was a statement he regretted making, and one he was certain hadn't worked until he heard a slight chuckle in the dark.

"Well, then everyone in my family should live forever." She announced through slight laughter.

"Yes." He was happy to hear her laugh, and he didn't want it to stop. "And, you'll outlive all of them."

More silence fell, until a hard punch was delivered to Reese's right shoulder in the dark. "I'm just driven." She announced before curling up to him in a world of uncertainty.

CHAPTER TWENTY-SIX

ALASKA

At 4:30 a.m. on Sunday, Enola woke to the steady to and fro of a dog tail, warning her that someone or something was just outside the Jeep, which prompted her to sit up and take his alert seriously. Her mouth dropped open at the sight of several caribou, probably ten feet from the Jeep, maybe twelve, an observation that prompted a serious question. *Why are so many animals making their way east?* That question had been churning in Enola's preliminary thought process since leaving Deadhorse, and now, as the two of them sat in the back of the Jeep, watching the reindeer, some nearly as tall as Enola, strutting in a timely fashion, with their white chests leading the way, the question became crystal clear. Enola and Miles watched their short tails fade into the distance. It wasn't until now, that Enola felt the unknown answer was probably serious. *Maybe the quake off Anchorage caused additional fires.* She imagined the faulty pipeline could have been caused by a shift in the earth's surface, and she rationalized that the closer they traveled to Fairbanks that additional sections of the pipeline could be damaged. *Maybe a small brush fire from a downed electrical line.* Her answers seemed logical, the part she didn't know about, or link to Wednesday's quake, was Miles' increased anxiety every time his paws met solid ground. She didn't know that all the animals were sensing continued seismic activity. She wasn't able to connect all the dots. For now, her mind convinced her that it was probably another fire, something she should keep an eye on as she made her way down the last fifty miles of the Dalton. *Watch for smoke and flame.* Her thoughts concluded.

Enola's Jeep climbed a rare stretch of asphalt, slowly. Wanting to soak in the endless mountain ranges and open tundra filled with tall thin stalks, some near_y six feet high, and topped with quarter-sized pink flowers (fireweed according to the woman at the Yukon Camp), Enola slowed her speed, so much so, that she was able to study the nearly transparent fireweed as the sun-kissed the back of each flower.

Flowers bloom low on the stalks first, then work their way to the top. That's when we know snow is just around the corner. Enola recalled the Yukon Camp woman's bittersweet information, a reminder that within the next couple of weeks, temperatures would plummet and snow would coat the entire Dalton with winter. It was a realization that brought tears down Enola's face. She knew her journey on the Dalton was ending, something she might never see again. It had changed her. She now understood, maybe with Dixie's help, that she couldn't allow loss to damage her. Like everything else in her life, it had to make her stronger. Becoming a frail-old-women, whose son hadn't seen or talked to her in twenty years, would have to be an occurrence where Enola could find gratitude. She couldn't afford for it to be any other way.

In full acceptance, Enola let the wind and dust blow in her driver's window during the last twenty miles, and tears she had spent the last fifteen minutes releasing on the Dalton turned into smiles, as her Jeep freely and gracefully bounced from one dip to another. Maneuvering sharp turns relaxed every part of her soul, a process she did slowly and passionately, and even after exiting the Dalton, she felt it inside of her.

She turned onto Old Elliott Highway in Livengood, as the sun settled into its three o'clock position. There weren't any services there, and she imagined there wouldn't be any people, except for the elderly man she had seen on her way up the Dalton, after realizing the road dead-ended, and after using the gravel lot to make a U-turn. It was an area that would normally remain unnoticed, and one that Enola would have missed if she hadn't seen the elderly man walking around the edge of an old wooden building in the far center, one overstocked with used tires and hubcaps. She imagined he was the owner of Hubcap Harrys, as he motioned in her direction, first with a friendly wave, followed by a relaxed smile, as she used his corner lot to make her way toward Dalton Highway. That was nine days ago; now, she was parked in the same location, where she made herself some hot soup, by using the one-burner propane stove that had served her well throughout the trip. It was a secluded cul-de-sac where she could walk Miles up and down the small road without worrying about other vehicles, not that she had seen any since Coldfoot, and a place where she could grab a short nap, before heading into Fairbanks, less than eighty miles away.

Just a one-hour catnap. Enola thought, before grabbing her golden selenite crystal from the small compartment near the Jeep's shifter and placing it between Miles and her stomach, which he was already snuggling against. *I can make Fairbanks before nightfall.* It was her last thought before shutting her eyes to Hubcap Harrys and the rest of the world.

CHAPTER TWENTY-SEVEN

ETHIOPIA

Abeba watched Mitch pull a crocodile out of the Shebelle River. She

stood under a large acacia tree, to stay out of the rain that hadn't

slowed since morning. The month of August had already been a

record-breaker for rainfall, nearly seven inches, in the small village,

and the month still had another six days left. Today was the twenty-

fifth, a day that the rain and sunshine played peek-a-boo with each other, and a day where the seventy-six-degree temperature warmed the damp atmosphere.

Abeba's dark skin glistened, a perfect contrast to the red fabric that played peek-a-boo with her tiny waist. The blanket styled wrap with tattered ends fell midway between her ankles and knees and was securely knotted in place just above her hips, exposing everything above her belly button, except what hid beneath a strand of red and green beads, which were loosely wrapped around her slender neck. She was intrigued by Mitch, his right arm working quickly, as he thrust it under the small crocodile's arm and held the back of the reptile's head with his hand, a replica of the half-Nelson he had perfected during high school wrestling, while his left hand quickly plunged his knife into the small area between the croc's eyes. Abeba counted the dead crocs on the riverbank. *Five.* Her calculation was in English. She smiled, knowing that it would be plenty, enough to feed the entire village at the feast, during tonight's Sunday evening celebration.

"Sahib, start carrying the crocs back to the village," Mitch ordered without thinking about the fact that each croc, even though small, weighted close to forty pounds, and then correcting his request, "see if you can get the ox-drawn cart hooked up and bring it as close as possible." Mitch made the request without hesitation, even though their presence in the small village had been less than twenty-four hours, they already felt like they were members of the tribe and were entitled to use all supplies and equipment.

"Okay, boss." Sahib tried to use white-man humor, something he had often heard his father do with white men who sometimes worked on a fishing boat near the coast, and something he hoped would get Abeba's attention flowing in his direction. He smiled after realizing it worked and slowed his jaunt to a slow stride when he sensed Abeba was following him. *I'll let her catch up.* Sahib thought privately before speaking. "Want to help me?" His question was aimed at Abeba, who had eagerly caught up with him. *She is beautiful.* The thought had been in Sahib's mind all morning. He wondered if she knew some English, like her father, Cadmar, the one in charge, and the one who Sahib's father had taught him would be referred to as the elder.

Sahib knew Abeba was four years older, but he was almost as tall, his eyes meeting her neckline, a dark golden chocolate, unflawed, like the rest of her. His eyes wanted to explore every inch of her, but he only allowed them to wander upward, taking in her forehead, which looked like it had been kissed by the sun, or he imagined, was the location on her body where pieces of her soul were escaping through her pores. He smiled at her oval-shaped face, one that seemed well paired with her lean torso, one that sprouted from the perfect neckline that he had been staring at, and one that lured his eyes to her lips, where his attention stagnated. Both the upper and lower were plump and full. He wondered if they had ever been kissed by more than the sun.

"Yes. I help." Abeba answered slowly, causing Sahib to quickly smile. Not only did she understand, but she spoke broken English. It was at that moment when Sahib knew he would someday marry Abeba. His smile faded when he thought about the process. The men in Daasanach villages can have several wives, but Sahib only wanted Abeba, and he would share her with no one. *First, I must buy her from Elder Cadmar.* Sahib thought privately, after remembering details from his father's teachings. *There will be a Dimi ceremony, where Abeba's father will be recognized as an elder, then Abeba, the love of my life, will be blessed for fertility and marriage.* Sahib's thoughts continued. *That's when I must be ready to buy Abeba from her father.*

"No!" The word escaped Sahib and left Abeba confused. "Yes." He corrected his outburst, after realizing he had reacted to the word *elder*, a title that he had heard others using in the village when addressing Elder Cadmar, Abeba's father. Then he asked the question before realizing that it would make his private thoughts obvious. "Are you circumcised?" He knew that was part of the Dimi Ceremony; he also knew that if Abeba had already been circumcised then she was already considered ready for marriage – now. He could tell by the confused look on her face that she didn't understand the word *circumcised*, so he formed a different question, one that would make his intentions clear. "Are you cut?"

"Yes," Abeba answered. "Make father proud."

Sahib disagreed, especially after hearing so many stories from his mother, about how the procedure caused many health risks, something he witnessed first-hand, when women in his village consulted his mother for care, because of severe pain or infection. He knew at least eighty percent of the females and males in Somalia were circumcised, and he knew it was something most members of the Daasanach Tribe did. The bloody ritual was something that infuriated Maryam. He had eavesdropped on his mother when she discussed the procedure with other mothers, as she tried desperately to talk them out of having it performed on their daughters, a gory operation where young girls would have a portion of their clitoris removed, if not the entire thing. Most boys in Africa were circumcised, something often done without any type of anesthetic medicine, a ritual usually performed around age thirteen. Sahib hadn't reached the age when it was typically done but knew even if he were still living with his mother, that she would never allow such a thing to happen. The thought made the foreskin on his penis quiver. It also made him feel bad for Abeba.

"You okay?" That was all he could think of to ask.

"Yes." She looked at him, without embarrassment, and after realizing he was concerned.

"We better hurry." He tried to refocus on the tasks at hand by remembering his goals: *get an ox-drawn cart, load crocs, deliver to village*, and then adding on a few private goals: *figure out how to get five or six cattle,* and then, *ask Elder Cadmar for his blessing.*

That night he sat with Mitch, the two of them centered around a large bonfire with other members of the village, a village they had become a part of.

"Mitch, she looks like an angel."

"Who?"

"Abeba."

"Do you like her?"

"She is going to be my wife." He whispered to Mitch's right ear.

"Really?" He smirked, not taking Sahib seriously.

"Yes." He had heard the doubt in Mitch's one-word question but would remain dauntless in his plan, the one that he rehearsed in his mind, while watching the smoke rise into the night sky.

It formed a nimbus above Abeba's head. It was a sign, one from his mother, Maryam. He knew she had sent Abeba down from heaven to be with him.

CHAPTER TWENTY-EIGHT

WASHINGTON STATE

Sunday was a cautiously lazy day. Cell phone towers in the nearby surrounding area were still down, and problems with the electrical grid on the western coast of Washington were still occurring. Thousands of people had been without power for five days. Allie and Reese had made it a point to stay out of sight from any other people, made it a point to keep their camper and Tahoe locked tight, and walked together along the back of the high school's property only as a necessity, mostly to allow the dogs to pee.

"You two kids okay?" The voice of an elderly woman could be heard from the other side of the fencing that separated the high school lot from the nearest street of houses. At first, Reese and Allie moved along, obscuring themselves within a patch of large oaks. They had both heard the question but imagined it was directed to members of her own family. "Can I ask you a question?" The elderly woman directed her voice down the fence line. Reese stopped, making out the woman's facial features through a six-foot-high fence that had been woven with green vinyl privacy slats. She was in her late seventies, had a posture that moved delicately and showed the fragility of her years, and a face that seemed colorless, with skin that appeared soft through wrinkles and lines.

"Yes, ma'am." Reese turned to face her, working his way closer to the fence.

"Do you know if the grocery store is going to open today?" She asked.

"I don't think they can until the electricity comes back on in this area."

Allie studied the woman. Her face looked weak, and she appeared shaky. She took her hand off the P22 that she had tucked in the back of her waistband, before speaking.

"Are you okay?" She redirected the woman's original question.

"I'm hungry." The woman smiled a slight smile. "I ran out of food two days ago." She used her hand to brush a stray gray hair back from her face. "None of my neighbors will answer the door." She looked at them. "The world has taken the last bit of trust from people." She looked as if she was trying not to cry.

Allie pulled Reese to the side, long enough for them to discuss their options: Ignore her pleas. Give the woman some food.

"We have food we can give you." Reese offered.

"I would appreciate that," the elderly woman said. "I can pay you back when the store opens." She looked at him. "I usually have food delivered every Wednesday, but the earthquake hit before they could get it to me."

"How will you cook it?" Allie asked, aware that the elderly woman probably didn't have a propane cooking stove like they did.

"I don't know." She sighed.

"Why don't you come eat with us?" The question was out before Allie realized what that would entail: driving the camper down the woman's road to pick her up and exposing themselves to any onlookers, but it was obvious she would never be able to walk down her street and around the back of the high school by herself. Her body was a feeble vessel leaving her tottering after each step.

"I could use the company," she answered. "I'm Margaret."

"I'm Allie." *We'll figure out a way.* Allie thought. "And this is Reese." They reached fingers between the open slats in the fence, allowing the woman to touch them. For a moment, Allie thought about human compassion during a crisis, wondered if someone was being kind to her own mother, and hoped the world would find its way back to a healthy normal. She missed being able to smile at strangers.

Reese studied the paint job on the house behind Margaret's left shoulder. A white house with pink trim. He tried to count the number of houses on the street, but his view was blocked by high fence line and more trees.

"We'll be over in twenty minutes to pick you up." He announced. "Could you stand just outside your front door?" he questioned while wondering how many other people would be watching them. No one else seemed to have gasoline in the area. No one. He knew that he and Allie had enough gas left in the Tahoe and in the two reserve cans to get them another three hundred miles if needed, and he wanted to keep it that way.

"Yes, I'll be ready." Margaret looked like a small amount of color came back into her face.

Allie and Reese took the dogs back to the camper, as they looked around for other people, but didn't see anyone. They didn't want to start the camper in broad daylight. It was a statement: We have gas and you don't. Allie had tried to keep an eye on other vehicles in the area. She hadn't noticed any of them move, and she hadn't noticed any sleepers since the interstate, but she knew they were out there. Lurking.

Reese warned Allie to keep the P22 low, and she agreed that she would sit in the car with the dogs, while Reese exited to meet Margaret at her doorstep. He noticed fingers pulling back curtains as he made his way down Tree Farm Lane. For a moment he felt boxed in, as he realized Margaret's house was on Tree Farm Court, a road that dead-ended on both ends and ran east to west, like the top line of a capital T.

"Stay alert." He warned Allie before making his way too far from the vehicle. Margaret was waiting on the front porch. Pink trim swirled like ribbons down the two pillars that announced her home. He approached her quickly; although, he was careful not to spook her, something that would be his last intention. "It's me Reese." He said to Margaret, before offering her his arm, an act that suggested she use it for balance.

It wasn't until the door opened behind her, that he realized they had been set up.

CHAPTER TWENTY-NINE

ALASKA

Paul Wabel was tired of defending his analysis, especially with people he had known for years.

"All I'm saying Paul is that according to your records, activity is now doubling around Mount Spurr." It was a friend, former anyway, that he had gone to high school with, and one that became a fierce competitor at the University of Anchorage, first within the science department, then in several classes which overlapped, some in geochemistry, and others in plate tectonics. Paul

Wabel always ended up a percentage or two higher. Always. Coming in second pissed O'Malley off, so much so, that he applied for the position of senior volcanologist and seismologist in Anchorage, just to spite Paul. It was a plan that backfired. Paul Wabel was a shoo-in, and the board members hardly gave Doug O'Malley a second thought. It was then that O'Malley decided to take a job on the east coast, an announcement he made at a holiday party, one that was supposed to make Paul Wabel jealous. It had the opposite effect, after O'Malley drunkenly bragged about his new job, unaware that the brother of his new boss was at the Christmas party, privy to the details, something that didn't register with O'Malley after consuming one too many beverages. *I'll be in charge of The World Disaster Division in D.C.* Paul recalled how Doug blew his own trumpet at the Christmas party, ten years back, just before he left. It was a boast that was promptly corrected across the banquet table.

Simon McKinney will be your boss. You'll be his assistant. The stern correction came from Simon McKinney's brother, as he mingled with guests near the head of the table. Doug O'Malley looked like he wanted to crawl under the banquet table and die. Paul

Wabel studied O'Malley's face, as he tried to keep his face expressionless. Ten years later he could still see the defeat on O'Malley's face, and ten years later Paul Wabel could still recall his immediate thought. *The fat fuck came in second again.*

Now, Doug O'Malley, *Assistant* Director at The World Disaster Division in Washington, D.C., was on the phone.

"I understand that Doug, but increased activity from Spurr can't cause another quake."

"I need you to be certain," Doug spoke with authority, to remind Paul that there were extreme measures that could be enacted, measures that would prevent another quake. Although controversial, *baiting,* a term that Doug O'Malley proudly coined to nickname a procedure that he had never been involved in, and one that he knew very little about, could be used to trigger an eruption inside Mount Spurr. Most scientists considered the mention of baiting absurd, but O'Malley who had earned a Doctoral in Volcanic Manipulation, a microscopic view covering volcanoes in Paul's opinion, was itching to commandeer a team of young scientists, placing them in a situation which would put their lives at risk, all to make a name for himself. Doug O'Malley had never even witnessed the procedure and had to go through an appeal process at the university, just to gain approval for using such an arguable topic for his thesis. And, it wasn't until after several failed attempts, spanning over the course of three months, each time filled with trial and error, that the delicate procedure had been deemed useful on a volcano in Hawaii, one that Paul imagined would only erupt every hundred years anyhow. *Bullshit thesis.* Paul laughed to himself after recalling O'Malley's dissertation.

Now, O'Malley was threatening to form a team and send them to Mount Spurr, to exercise the highly unorthodox procedure of lowering detonation devices into the belly of Mount Spurr, literally causing it to erupt, making it less probable to erupt in the next fifty years or so. *Baiting is a fucking stupid name.* Paul Wabel's thoughts also included unbiased reality: *it would cost Anchorage millions of dollars in clean up and restoration, and it would end up costing lives.* He stopped his thoughts after he realized O'Malley was talking.

"Anchorage can't afford to be hit with another quake right now. Buildings and bridges are weak from the 7.2 *we* just got slammed with, and you know as well as I do, that the probability of the next one being bigger is over eighty percent, if it occurs within the next thirty days."

"Yes Doug. I know the facts." He took a deep breath before constructively addressing his class nemesis, someone who always took friendly competition too seriously in his opinion. "Fact one: There is no *we*. Don't forget your loyalties are to the east coast now." The stupid son-of-a-bitch hadn't lived in Anchorage in over ten years. "Fact two: Don't forget my doctoral degree was in Volcanic Simulation." His tone was sarcastic, as his word choice mocked O'Malley's degree in Volcanic Manipulation. He looked at the wall in his office, the same one that held his doctoral degree from The University of Anchorage – Doctorate in Seismic Science. "If Mount Spurr erupts, it will not cause a quake." Now his tone was serious. "As much as the public wants to believe it, there is no correlation Doug." He sighed. "I guess you believe in the fucking Easter Bunny too."

"Okay, Paulie." Paul Wabel hated being called Paulie. That was something only his mother got away with. "I'll hold off on forming a team to address Mount Spurr."

"You do that Dougie. Oh, and say hello to your boss for me; you know, the one that has the authority to make such a fucking asinine decision." Paul wished he could see O'Malley's face through the satellite phone.

"Fuck you." O'Malley got the last two words in, before quickly disconnecting. Wabel smiled knowing the phone wasn't the only thing dead between them, so was the minimal friendship.

#

Sunday evening, Paul Wabel stopped by the small florist off Benson Boulevard to get a bouquet of yellow and white daisies, his mother's favorite. Every other Sunday, he would visit his mother's grave. She had insisted on being buried, so she would have a direct view of *Sleeping Lady* from the cemetery overlooking Cook Inlet. Paul didn't believe in wasting space with cadavers but didn't want to alter his mother's wishes.

Paulie, make sure I can see Sleeping Lady. He could still hear his mother's dying words, not the ones he wanted to hear, just another act of pretense in a world already overloaded with make-believe. *I will mother.* He felt her hand go limp; time had run out to hear the words he needed most: Paulie you are a good son; Paulie I love you; or even, Paulie I'm proud of you for getting a doctoral degree. He was glad she had beaten the odds and cruelty of Parkinson's disease long enough to be transported by shuttle and wheelchair to his graduation ceremony, but even that night was filled with disappointment. Instead of congratulating him, and instead of using the hour to spend quality time with her son before being shuttled back to the assisted living residential care program, she wanted to stop by the park at Cook Inlet, so she could stare across the water to watch the setting sun melt into Sleeping Lady.

Nonetheless, he loved his mother and respected her fairytale lifestyle, so much so, that he made sure her collection of over 200 Sleeping Lady statues and wall portraits ended up in the museum in downtown Anchorage, minus the one he kept for himself, one he had made into a large canvas print, a reminder of the photo she had requested he snap, when the sun fell gently on Sleeping Lady, a souvenir of the hour he had spent with his mother overlooking Cook Inlet, after receiving his doctoral degree. Staring out at Sleeping Lady and taking a photo wasn't an activity he wanted to do, but it was something his mother enjoyed, like a bouquet of fresh daisies.

"I love you Mom." He said the words to her headstone, as he placed the bouquet of yellow and white daisies in the flower holder, and after removing last week's bouquet, one that had hardened in the Anchorage sunlight. "Sleeping Lady is still watching us." He remarked, before turning and walking away.

CHAPTER THIRTY

WASHINGTON STATE

Enola had taught Allie to believe in good luck, to worship the

horseshoe-shaped symbol, something they each had in their

collection of wall art – a rusty piece of metal, originals found when

Allie was eight years old, during a summer trip to North Carolina to

visit Dixie and Ryan. It was the same summer Enola took both Mitch

and Allie on an excursion to a cabin in Marshall, a small town in

Madison County, North Carolina. Sitting at the top of a mountain, one the locals called Woodrow Wilson, dense thicket hid the secret hide-a-way, a cabin used by Dacey and Melantha Fears for several years when Enola was a kid. It was an unmentioned summer getaway, and the only place Enola felt safe during her childhood. It had been a place where Enola could lose herself in sixty acres of loblolly pine, black cherry, walnut, sweetgum and magnolia, the hindmost still a sweet lemony smell in Enola's soul. It would always be part of her, just like the crisp mountain streams, which then served as borders from the abusive man that she believed was her biological father and the mentally collapsed woman she wished could function as her mother. It was a place that would always be part of Enola's inner being, a seed that planted good fortune.

But now, it wasn't a time to rely on luck; the present situation in front of Allie needed action. She exited the front passenger seat of the Tahoe, after pulling the keys out of the ignition, and shoving them under the seat, before leaving the vehicle's door wide open behind her. Three anxious dogs waited for commands to follow: one full-bred pit bull, one lab, and one mix, a result of the first two, and just as large as his parents. "Stay." She ordered.

She walked slowly toward the house with large decorative columns, carefully planting each foot so she wouldn't stumble, and cautiously keeping the Walther P22 semiautomatic steady in her extended left hand, with her right bracing for a shot.

"Get away from him." Allie was ready to shoot. "Back the fuck up." Her demand became more specific. "Into the house." She imagined her first shot would take out the large asshole that stood behind Margaret. He had to be at least 275 pounds, with a gross amount of body fat, each pound of which had taken a threatening step toward Reese. "Don't make me do it." She held her aim steady.

Margaret's son stopped long enough to stare down Allie. Unrattled, she studied his pinpoint pupils, each set in a mud-brown iris that floated between crepey upper eyelids and lower eyelids that looked swollen and puffy. He appeared to be in his late fifties, but Allie imagined he looked ten years older than his actual age, because of his obvious drug problem. He took one step back from Reese, but quickly recalculated his options, administering a hard-right hook to the left side of Reese's face. Before Allie could get off a shot, Reese and the man who had just pissed him off were tangled in an endless wrestling match on the front porch. Allie kept the gun pointed at Margaret, who had taken a couple of steps back. Pointing a gun at an elderly woman was not something Allie wanted to do, but it was obvious the woman could no longer be trusted. Margaret stood in a mixture of shock and disbelief, watching her son's massive build take several blows to the head and face. He quickly became disoriented and unable to fight back, as Reese delivered a final blow, but not before Allie gave the command to the three dogs that anxiously waited.

"Zeus, Shiloh, Yoda, attack!" They had surrounded the dazed and useless mass of human flesh within seconds and didn't stop barking until instructed. Zeus was wound the tightest, after watching the action unfold, and took a hard bite out of the man's nipple, a flabby mound of skin that protruded under the man's white t-shirt, and one that was suddenly turning a bright red. Blood flowed freely down the man's upper torso.

"He bit me in the fucking chest!" Margaret's son exclaimed. The pain was sharp, even though he had swallowed six Oxycontin pills less than two hours earlier with a warm beer.

"You're lucky I didn't put a bullet in your chest." Allie followed up, giving the forty-eight-year-old a look that warned him she was still considering it, and one that made Margaret and her useless adult son follow the first directive she had given – *in the house* – as the two of them turned their backs to the gun and walked inside.

Allie made the mother-son duo sit down on the living room sofa, a process that allowed her enough time to take notice of the open pantry, one loaded with canned goods, boxed Hamburger Helper, rice dishes, peanut butter, canned meats, bottled water, and several bags of beef jerky, and long enough to ask the question she had on her mind.

"What were you going to take from us?" Allie demanded. Her question aimed at both of them. The overweight asshole didn't have a brain in his head, which his smart-ass answer confirmed.

"I was planning on killing him and having my way with you." His crude announcement filled her with anger. "I saw you walking the dogs." He paused, but then continued like a six-year-old who didn't know better than to ramble on with the truth. "You're pretty." His comment was directed at Allie, but his disappointed eyes turned to his mother, seated beside him, someone that continually supported him with her monthly checks, and someone that enabled his every move, no matter how vile. "Momma was supposed to set the snare like I used to do to catch birds." Allie saw the fifth-grade mentality reek from his dark eyes. She was using every ounce of control she had not to shoot them both right then and there.

"I'm sorry," Margaret announced. "My son has a problem." Her apology lacked sincerity.

"Allie, let's go." Reese was shaking, not out of fear, but anger. He knew taking the lives in front of him would be doing society a favor, but he wasn't that type of person, not unless it was a last resort. He replayed the emotionally delayed man's words in his head, thinking about how this could have played out, and reassuring himself that he wouldn't hesitate to take the man's life to protect Allie. "Let's leave them." He said. "We will call the cops and report this piece of shit when the cell towers work again."

"Grab two trash bags." That was Allie's response. Her voice fought for control, as she pointed to the box of black Kirkland trash bags on the counter, the one sitting directly behind several prescription bottles of God-knows-what. "Please." She added, remembering she wasn't mad at Reese.

Reese stepped around Shiloh, Zeus, and Yoda, who looked like hired guard dogs and were ready to pounce as directed, before grabbing two bags, then turning back around to look at Allie. "What did you want these for Allie?" He held his breath while she answered, wondering if she had plans to hurt the deviant and his mother, something he knew had crossed his mind.

"Fill the bags with water, canned goods, boxed food, and the beef jerky." She thought about how many young girls and women he had probably hurt in his lifetime; it wasn't realistic to think she would have been the first. "Hand me those prescription bottles." She said. Reese had just finished clearing the pantry, holding both bags with one hand, and grabbed the medication bottles with the other: one was labeled Oxycontin and the other was labeled Vicodin.

"Please hold this." Allie loosened her grip on the P22, after freeing Reese's hand of the prescription bottles, then disappeared into the hall bathroom, where Shiloh followed her. Reese heard the toilet flush twice. Allie made her way back down the hall, stopping long enough to peer in the man's bedroom. Photos of young girls, partially clothed, hung around his headboard, causing Allie to regret her decision, the one where she had decided to let the piece of shit live.

It wasn't until she returned with the empty pill bottles, tossing them at the sexual predator, that his reaction made her think she was finally going to get her wish. He stood. The entire front of his shirt was tie-dyed red from Zeus' attack outside on the porch. Catching on to what Allie had done with his pills, he took a step forward, again swinging, this time toward Allie's head, but clearly missing.

Reese fired once, just above the fat man's skull, missing the top of his head intentionally. *Seven more bullets.* He thought. *All of them will go in next time.* "Are you okay?" He asked Allie, wondering if it would be wrong to just kill him. Zeus had apparently wondered the same thing and had decided to take action, even though he hadn't been given the go-ahead. He lunged over the coffee table that separated him from the man, spilling over a half-empty beer can, and knocking the man into a sitting position on the couch, before taking off what was left of the bloody nipple.

Allie and Reese called him off, but only after several minutes had passed. Leaving the mother hovering over her son's injuries, they left the house with two black plastic bags full of pantry items and three large black dogs. They didn't hurry. They simply walked to the vehicle, ordered the dogs to get inside, fished the car keys out from under the passenger seat where Allie had placed them and drove off. This time it was Allie in the driver's seat. Turning the camper around on small streets was her specialty, and finding her way across the Canadian border was her mission.

They jumped on 542 East until they saw Everson Goshen Road, where Allie decided to make a firm right. Confident she was heading north, she traveled eighteen minutes, while Reese silently formulated a plan that he thought she'd listen to.

"We don't know for sure where your mother is." He said. "I get that you want to travel into Canada the way she went in." He followed up. "But we need a plan." The answer was straight ahead. "Let's stop here for the evening." He suggested, pointing to Sumas RV Park. "I know we're less than five miles away from the border."

She looked at him, trying to contain the frustration in her eyes – frustration from having no phone service, frustration from having no contact with her mother, frustration from having to protect themselves against the dregs of society, and frustration that they were caught up in the aftermath of an earthquake. She wanted everything to go back to normal: daily text messages or calls from her mother, electricity, food, water, gasoline, and people that weren't out to hurt others just because a natural disaster paved the way for greater opportunity. She knew Reese was right. She couldn't approach border patrol half-cocked. A plan was mandatory.

She slowed, after pulling into the Sumas RV Park, and then came to a stop in front of the office. Nightly rates were forty-dollars, although that included power which wasn't available. "Maybe we can talk them down to twenty," Allie said, before noticing the sign

on the door. OFFICE CLOSED.

"Let's find a designated site," Reese suggested. "If

someone's here in the morning, we'll settle up."

"Okay." Allie touched Reese's hand, feeling his inner

strength, something she wanted to rely on, at least for tonight. She

pulled into a spot marked for a long RV, one across from the

bathhouse, which she hoped would at least offer a cold shower. Her

outer skin yearned for moisture and her insides hungered for more

than a hot meal. She craved peace. It was an itch that was gently

soothed by the black and white tuxedo cat who purred near her head,

after showers, after devouring a large bowl of Betty Crocker's

Hamburger Helper minus meat, and after watching three brave dogs

eat their well-deserved rations of kibble.

The mound of black and white fur unknowingly became a

preliminary headliner for the thoughts that tossed and turned in her

mind throughout the night. *Survival is not a black-and-white issue.* It

was a comparison that filled her restless mind. She knew the line that separates right and wrong had widened, and she knew the recent events had affected people's actions, even her own. *Is killing another human being sometimes warranted? Is stealing justified when trying to survive? What actions are condoned?*

The questions stayed with her throughout the night, as well as Zeus, who never left her side. Neither did the P22.

CHAPTER THIRTY-ONE

ETHIOPIA

On Monday, Mitch woke during the early morning fog to the sound

of a nail gun being carelessly and rapidly sprayed over the small

village. He listened. *It isn't a nail gun; it is a lot more unforgiving.*

He had heard the racket before. *Ak-47.* The movie that came to his

mind was *Scarface*, starring Al Pacino, a look into the world of a

drug cartel, and one that had debuted six years before he was even

born, but one his father, Rex Narducci, had repeatedly watched with

him, after finally agreeing to take Allie and Mitch on alternating weekends, following the divorce from Enola, and after three-year-old Allie would fall asleep, leaving Rex in a frantic search to entertain an eight-year-old boy who had lost faith in him.

Mitch's mind separated fact from fiction. *This isn't a movie,* he reminded himself. *It is real.* After accepting the reality, his mind processed the tail end of more gunfire. *PAAAP.* He digested the hubbub slowly. Screaming echoed in its aftermath, followed by shouting. Two, maybe three men's voices, filled the Ethiopian village. Mitch recognized the deepest tone. It was Elder Cadmar's unwavering voice; Mitch recognized its strength. It was the language he couldn't decipher; although, he felt certain the baritone dialect wasn't meeting the gunman's satisfaction, after hearing an additional thirty rounds of firepower spray over the small village. His first reaction was to duck. His second was to search the other side of the hut for Sahib, a much-needed translator, but his eyes grew disappointed after he found the wooden platform-style bed littered with straw and blankets, but no body. Sahib was gone. Before he could process his roommate's disappearance, his thoughts were overpowered by the elder's voice once again. This time Mitch recognized a slight difference in the elder's tone. He knew the

gunman had weakened Cadmar by threatening to wreak devastation

on the small village. *He's caving in.* Mitch didn't need to understand

the unfamiliar language; he knew what was going on. *Cadmar*

doesn't see a way out.

He pulled his knife from the leather sheath, still in the spot

where his head had rested minutes earlier, and using his knife, he cut

his way through the back of the hut. Keeping his legs hidden behind

the strategically placed wooden stilts, he maneuvered behind several

other huts, knife in hand, and finally positioned himself behind the

hut where Elder Cadmar was standing. He looked for dead or injured

villagers but could tell by the condition of the once neatly layered

grass and bamboo roofs, that the subject of the two men's anger had

been taken out on structures, not people, at least not yet.

He watched the young tribal man holding the Ak-47 move

closer to Elder Cadmar. His tone was threatening and exhibited little

patience. Mitch could see the seriousness in his eyes, even from the

spot where he remained hidden. The shooter's eyebrows curved

slightly, as his face showed his anger, resulting in several exaggerated lines just above the bridge of his nose. His hands remained steady, ready to pull the trigger. Mitch calmly studied the situation. The dark-skinned tribal man, couldn't have been a day over twenty-five years old, weighed somewhere around 130 pounds, and held an Ak-47 with a long black barrel, one appearing at least sixteen inches, steady with one hand in front of the curved magazine, and one hand behind it. Mitch noticed the empty magazine on the ground near the shooter's feet. He imagined it was the magazine that had been emptied in rapid-fire as a warning. The new magazine was locked and loaded into place and was pointed at Cadmar's skull.

Mitch thought about simply walking forward. Then he thought about running full speed, knife in hand, taking the shooter out before his finger could pull the trigger. He knew there would be a risk either way. *Where the fuck is Sahib?* He wondered. Wishing he was near to interpret the dialogue that was being exchanged within earshot. *Where the fuck did the other man go?* His mind remembered registering two male voices in a heated debate with Cadmar. Not one. It bothered him that he had never established visual contact with the second intruder. *Where was he?* Mitch questioned himself quietly, as he turned his head and body, his eyes searching a 360-degree circle from the back left-hand corner, behind the hut. Nothing. Everyone in the village seemed to be out of sight, except for Elder Cadmar. Then Mitch heard the voice of Abeba. She had quietly approached from behind.

"Save father." She whispered.

"Where is Sahib?" He questioned, ignoring her request.

Before she could respond, Mitch heard the second male intruder's voice call from a patch of African juniper trees. He repeated an unfamiliar phrase in a rattled excitement, one that became louder, the closer he got to his accomplice. He had a firm grip on Sahib's arm, pushing him toward the gunman.

"Hata-hatta. Hata-hatta. Hata-hatta." The second dark-skinned tribal member shouted without taking a breath. Mitch looked at Abeba for translation.

"Steal. Steal. Steal." Abeba whispered. Then before Mitch could ask her for more details, she added information. "Cow." Mitch wondered why Sahib would steal a cow from another village. "Six." She held up all five digits on one hand and one more on her other.

"Cows." Mitch corrected her use of a singular noun, more out of frustration. *Why the fuck would Sahib steal six cows from another village?* He knew Elder Cadmar's village was sufficiently feeding its tribe. There was no reason to steal from another village.

"Sahib marry me," Abeba answered Mitch's question without it being asked. Mitch had seen the chemistry between Abeba and Sahib, had listened to Sahib explain the purpose of last night's feast, a celebration for Elder Cadmar and Abeba, commemorating Abeba's readiness to become a wife, and had even listened to him explain that it was customary for suitors to approach the elder with cattle to marry his daughter.

"I should have seen this coming." This time Mitch's frustration was directed at himself, as he watched the man who had a grip on Sahib release him, after pushing him in front of the shooter, then quickly turning around to rope the six small calves that had worked their way up from the patch of junipers. Abeba's already stressed breaths became exacerbated over Mitch's right shoulder when they both watched the shooter take the Ak-47 off Abeba's father and place the long black steel against Sahib's right temple.

Mitch thought about his sister Allie, and his mother Enola, as he looked on. He knew Abeba's heart was breaking. He recalled Sahib's endless conversation around the bonfire last night, the one where he had explained the Daasanach tribe's belief system about death. He remembered Sahib pointing to the smoky halo above Abeba's head, the one that made her look like an angel, and the one that he was sure was a sign from his dead mother, Maryam.

"The Daasanach believe my mother's soul is somewhere safe." He had told Mitch as they sat around the bonfire. "They believe souls live in a safe place until the person can be healthy again."

"Like reincarnation?" Mitch asked.

"I'm not sure what that is," Sahib said in the night sky.

"Reborn?" Mitch followed up.

"Yes," Sahib said. "Like that." Then added. "Never die."

Mitch stood, knife ready, then ran at the gunman full speed.

He never stopped, even after hearing gunshots.

CHAPTER THIRTY-TWO

WASHINGTON STATE

On Monday, at 1:24 in the morning, Washington State time, Allie sat up. Her world was shaking again. Only five days had passed since last week's three quakes and two tsunamis, one of which made Allie and Reese leave a place they were beginning to call home. Now, it was happening again.

Paul Wabel knew about the early morning quake right away, first because Anchorage shook harder than it ever had since he was born. He had studied the printout, carefully calculated its severity, several times, making sure the Richter scale was correct. 9.3. He knew it had topped the 1964 Alaskan earthquake, one that his mother had lived through before he existed; it had taken the lives of her best friend's father and brother, along with another 129 people. Paul knew it was bad, as it had violently bounced him off the leather sofa in his office and onto the floor before he even knew what was happening.

Allie woke, her body still twitching, after the rolling motion roused her from sleep, interrupting her dream, one where she had just finished swimming in Little Lake Thomas alongside Mitch, her brother, where she had been soaking up Florida rays that fought the banyan tree's leathery leaves that towered above the lake's edge, finding a passageway to Allie's four-year-old arms, as they reached and pulled water to keep her head above the alligator-infested lake. *I won't let one get you Allie.* She could still hear her brother's reassuring tone as he talked to her about how easy it was to fight one off. It wasn't until Mitch's ten-year-old voice faded, that she realized decades had passed, an unwanted reality that brought her back to the here and now. She opened her eyes, allowing her mind to gather details – Sumas RV Park, close to the Canadian border. She felt displaced. Florida was only a memory, so was Seaside, where similar visions had played in her mind before drifting off to sleep. Those were of her and Reese. Her body floated on a small rubber raft near the water's edge, underneath an Oregon sky, while Reese tossed a frisbee along the shoreline to dogs that competed for possession. Now, even those more recent memories seemed gone forever. Her life had permanently changed, as a result of last week's events, and now, as her world felt unsteady, she knew it would change even more. *Survival is not a black-and-white issue.* She recalled bits and pieces of the conversation she shared with Reese, from the night before when they hurried through cold showers, an exchange she held responsible for the tossing, turning, and dreaming that had plagued her throughout the night, and internal chitchat that was currently egging her parietal lobe into action, encouraging her thoughts to interpret the earth's movement. *What if the world is ending?*

"Hold tight." It was Reese's voice that stopped her from pondering the question any longer. His arm held her close after he realized she was thrashing in an unsettled world. "You're okay." Those words were enough to prompt her body into sitting upright, her face meeting Zeus' square jawline. His space was limited, after first allowing Shiloh and Yoda on the full-size mattress, and even though the three full-size canines most certainly could, each one was careful not to step on Serenity who had wedged herself between Allie and Reese in the middle of the night.

"What the hell is going on?" She asked Reese, who had pushed himself into a sitting position beside her.

"I think it was another quake." He answered. "I don't know where." He composed himself. "I just know it was strong and seemed to roll the ground beneath us."

"I want to go outside." She announced, her breathing was stressed. "I *need* to go outside." Reese knew going outside wasn't the best thing to do, but he felt like the ground had finally stopped tottering, and he wasn't going to let her go by herself, so he conceded, first by standing, then by reaching for her hand.

Looking up at the night sky that hadn't reached two a.m., she felt helpless, realizing her mother was probably still two thousand miles away, and knowing that the shaking was probably the result of another Alaskan quake, creating a world where her mother's well-being could be compromised.

"She's okay." Reese didn't know what else to say to Allie's darkened face, one that glistened with tears, under the moonlight. "It had to be close." He thought about the movement that he had felt. *Wobbling. Swaying. Tumbling.* "It couldn't be Alaska again. It felt nearby." He was trying to think logically.

Allie imagined he was right, her mind calculating the distance between Sumas, Washington and the center of Alaska. *Too far.* She let her thoughts settle before speaking. "Maybe it was off the Washington coast this time." She was listening for sound. Nothing. Just silence.

"I just hope the west coast is not hit with another tsunami." Reese was trying to agree with Allie's location, by directing her thoughts down the west coast, anywhere but Alaska. "I guess there's nothing we can do tonight." He made the observation, hoping it would prompt Allie into stepping back inside, out from under the empty night sky.

"I want to do a walk around." She answered his attempt. "Just to check for damage." He followed her lead, first checking the left side of the camper and Tahoe, then the front of the Tahoe, then the right side of the camper and Tahoe, and finally the back of the camper. Everything seemed intact.

"We'll do a better check come daylight." He suggested.

"Okay." She stepped inside, where all of the animals were still planted on the full-sized mattress, waiting.

The next six hours were filled with various sleep patterns: one dog at each head and one at Reese's feet with Serenity in the middle, one dog at each set of feet and one dog above Reese's head with Serenity tangled in Allie's hair, and upon waking, two dogs in the middle, with Serenity under Allie's right arm, and Zeus standing at the foot of the bed, where he locked eyes with Allie's brown ones when she woke.

Fifteen minutes later, they did another walk around. No damage, then slowly drove toward the Canadian border, without a plan. Parking the Tahoe and camper off to the side, Allie insisted on going inside the front door of the border patrol office. It was a move she hadn't rehearsed, but one she felt compelled to do.

"May I help you?" The dark eyes looked at her, his stubbled chin moving with each word.

"My mother is making her way back to this crossing from Alaska." She announced, thinking on her feet. "Can we cross over with proper I.D., just to meet her, then we'll do what's necessary to get passports to return to the United States side?" It was a tangled question, but one she felt like asking, even though she knew the policy had changed over the years. No longer could you enter Canada without a passport. Nonetheless, she just wanted a response.

Something. The dark-eyed man looked at her, studying the concern in her face, and tried to word his answer as delicately as possible.

"Did you feel the surge last night?" He asked, hoping her answer would lead him in the right direction.

"Yes, it woke us up," she answered, appreciating the man's friendly demeanor while analyzing his use of the word *surge*. "It was another quake," she announced as if her information had already been verified. "Probably off the coast of Washington this time." It was a theory that both Reese and Allie had agreed to.

"There was another earthquake last night. Fourth one the globe has seen in less than a week, but the rolling motion you felt wasn't from the new quake." The two-day shadow announced. "It was from a massive amount of water being sucked back and released." He confidentially answered. "We could feel the pull and release way over here, sort of a rocking motion." He announced.

"So, there was another tsunami also?" Allie asked the source of information in front of her. He confirmed by nodding.

"Yes. It was a trifecta last night," he said. "First a volcanic eruption, then a massive earthquake, topped off with a tsunami," he informed her.

"Where did all this happen?" Reese asked the question for Allie. He knew she was just trying to hold herself together.

"All three hit Anchorage," he answered. Allie tried to process the information without imagining the worse, but the details that followed painted Allie's face with despair. "Some people are saying it's a sign." He announced. "You know – Father, Son, and Holy Ghost." The man tilted his head slightly to the side, his body language signaling that he believed it could be a possibility. Reese could feel Allie's blood run cold through her skin. "It is hard to believe that a volcanic eruption, an earthquake, and a tsunami hit one area. I guess it all started around midnight in Anchorage, a few minutes after one a.m. our time," The man continued. "Anchorage is a mess." He followed up. "The roads between here and Alaska are undisturbed, but Alaska is a war zone. Volcanic ash went hundreds of miles, and the quake was a big one. They're saying it topped the 1964 quake. Maybe a 9.3." He stopped for a moment, after noticing the deadpan look that stared back at him. "I can't let you through without a passport anyway, but I have to tell you the roads aren't drivable around Anchorage, and they're extremely dangerous around Fairbanks."

"How did the quake affect Fairbanks?" Reese stepped in once again, knowing Allie wasn't able to speak. Not now.

"Several landslides have been reported." It was the last thing Allie heard before her knees hit the laminate flooring.

CHAPTER THIRTY-THREE

ALASKA

Triaphilia. Paul Wabel knew there was an actual name for the belief
that some people hold close to their hearts, a belief where bad things
happen in sets of three. *Superstitious bullshit.* His thoughts followed
O'Malley's call, a call that occurred just after midnight, after
printouts documenting Spurr's eruption was assessable on both the
west coast and east coast, and after his see-I-told-you-so phone call
lasted through the massive earthquake that followed.

"I fucking told you this would happen." Doug O'Malley's drunken voice filled the satellite phone in Wabel's office, where he struggled to keep his footing, while his eyes alternated back and forth between the seismograph report with thick black lines and the Richter scale report. *A 9.3*. With quivering hands, he repositioned each report, nearly forgetting that Doug O'Malley was still on the other end of the satellite phone that was wedged between the ball of his upper right shoulder and his right ear; although he wasn't listening to O'Malley's rant and rave. Angling one report at a time toward the hall light where the emergency generator had kicked on, Paul's disbelieving eyes studied the earthquake report, while his mind made the comparison to the 1964 quake, one that had occurred seventy-four miles southeast of Anchorage, and one that had caused over three million dollars in damage, a figure that the mathematical side of him knew would plummet over two billion today.

Still holding the satellite phone in place with his shoulder, and still letting O'Malley babble, he made his way to his desk, where his lamp had now popped on, courtesy of the computer system that directed the generator to supply light in occupied offices.

My poor baby. He comforted himself, hoping the report about Spurr was a mistake. It wasn't; he had the proof right in front of him, first on the paper he was holding, and second on his office window, where thick ash currently obstructed his view of Cook Inlet. He knew hot ash had traveled hundreds of miles in all directions because one of his children had thrown a temper tantrum, one that had been followed by the largest quake Paul had known in his lifetime.

Realizing that the fat Irish fuck was still shouting, he listened. Paul expected to hear slurred speech about sloppy data, tectonic plates, volcanic triggers, underground wells, hydraulic fracturing, or even global changes. What he did not expect to hear was drunk talk about number mysticism.

"Three is the first odd prime number Paulie." His voice was garbled. "It's a pattern. Point 33333333…." Doug Wabel disconnected before letting him finish his ongoing and incessant threes.

Standing, Doug walked toward the large picture window in his office and rubbed his hand on the tempered safety glass; his first thought was to clear a spot for vision, followed by the realization that the ash was on the outside. It was a reaction that any parent would have. He thought about walking outside for a view but knew it wouldn't be safe, so he allowed himself to pace alongside the thickly covered window, one where he normally had a view of Sleeping Lady and his surrounding volcanoes. Even at night, the Pacific coast moonlight offered a view of their silhouettes in a clear sky.

Now, he could only imagine. Ash kept Anchorage's fate hidden. He knew it was bad out there, and imagined the glass that separated him from the rest of the world was one of the few pieces that hadn't crumbled under the 9.3 quake, a monster, just topping the one his mother lived through in her early twenties. He understood now, why she was so obsessed with Sleeping Lady, needing something tangible to protect a city that had been shaken to its knees. *131 dead.* He remembered her eyes when she'd talk about the 1964 quake. *Fear. Sadness. Loss.* Now, it had happened again.

He settled into his executive leather office chair, waiting for more phone calls to begin, and in an attempt to regain his composure. Mentally he was exhausted; he knew it by the way his eyes couldn't stay focused. Staring at the wall in front of him, he placed his thumb about ten inches in front of his face and tried to focus on it. He knew the exercise, one meant to get his eyes to focus, would work better with a blank wall in front of him; instead of one with the large canvas of Mount Susitna. It was a fact that made him jump to his feet, after realizing the large canvas print wasn't even there. It had literally bounced off the wall, either as a result of the volcanic eruption or earthquake, or both. *Goddammit.* His foul language was out of frustration. He never realized until that moment how much he liked the large canvas photograph of Sleeping Lady, one that made him think of his mother every time he looked at it. He hurried to the canvas, which lay with one corner touching drywall a couple feet off the ground, and another corner near baseboard trim. The other two corners swayed like a teeter-totter in mid-air, over a small space heater, one that had sharp metal vents.

His hands reached for the painting. *Mount Susitna.* He said her real name, as his fingers rubbed across the front of the canvas, checking for punctures. None. He hated that the view he normally had of her was still obstructed by ash at the moment. He had requested a large picture window when the contractors designed his office, one that would give him an optimal view of Mount Susitna. He convinced himself over the last five years that it was to honor his mother, and not to support any childhood bullshit.

Still, he knew his mind would be at ease if he could only see her, sleeping soundly across Cook Inlet. He walked near the large picture window once again, where just by sound, he could tell there were nimbus clouds above the already battered city, as he listened to the large drops of water hit the outside window ledge. Hard. He closed his eyes, as feelings of empathy overwhelmed him, a result of visualizing the people of Anchorage fighting another week filled with devastating acts of nature. *Volcanic eruption. Earthquake. Severe rain. Three fucking catastrophes in one night.* He thought of Doug O'Malley. *Fat fuck. Maybe things do come in threes.* Although, the scientific side of him knew it wasn't uncommon for rainfall to occur during or after an eruption; he also knew that it wasn't enough to settle Spurr's belly. The damage was done, and now the rainfall would just add to the mess, creating a mixture of mud and rock fragments, another threat to the area around Spurr. *The mix, known as lahar, can cause violent mudslides.* Then, after trying to put his scientific thoughts to rest, at least for a moment, he studied the view across the inlet. Lining up his eyes with a rain-washed opening whose view imitated a kaleidoscope, he angled his head. First to get a panoramic of Spurr, whose position in the darkened sky was covered by thick polluted air – a mixture of ash and debris that would fill the sky for weeks on end, and keep her hidden, with the exception of a steady stream of lava, that Paul Wabel's eyes were processing. *There must be a new fissure on the east side of Spurr.* He tried to picture its location.

It was an emotional sight, one he would accompany his team to during their next trip so that he could see the damage up close, after he felt it was safe. He needed information, and he needed to place his feet on Spurr, one of his 452 children, and one that he knew was crying for attention.

The downpour of rain cleaned more ash off the outside of his office window, allowing Paul to get a better view across Cook Inlet. It had even cleared part of the dark ashy sky, allowing enough moonlight to bleed over Spurr and the surrounding area. Paul Wabel's eyes took advantage before backing away from his office window, hoping to survey the damage, and hoping to catch a glimpse of Mount Susitna. He stared long and hard at Sleeping Lady, hoping his already stressed eyes were deceiving him. His hands searched for the inside window ledge, its four-inch sill offering some support for his trembling fifty-two-year-old arms as he allowed his mind to accept the view across Cook Inlet. *Her head is gone.* He imagined a thick concoction of mud and debris had washed it into the surface below. *Lahar.* He tried to focus on a scientific explanation, anything to avoid thinking about his mother's words: *Sleeping Lady lies on the other side of Cook Inlet and watches over you. Paulie, you will always be safe, unless she crumbles to her death, then you must run for safety.*

At 12:44, Paul Wabel watched a wall of water hit his third-floor office window. The weighty impact of wind and water penetrated the large window frame. Shattered pieces of glass fought to stay within the laminate membrane, but like Sleeping Lady, the outline gave way.

Paul Wabel's self-awareness died the moment his brain stopped working. He had never believed in a God-given soul, and the scientific side of him had spent his adulthood processing death – a power supply that stops functioning.

CHAPTER THIRTY-FOUR

ETHIOPIA

Less than thirty seconds passed before Mitch was tackling the gunman. He had waited until the shooter repositioned the Ak-47, aiming it low, and randomly spraying bullets near Sahib's feet, as his laughter grew while watching the young boy's anxiety. Mitch didn't hesitate, after making sure his knife was firmly gripped in his right hand, his legs quickly imitated the explosive movements of an NFL running back, promptly placing him behind the gunman, before his approach was even noticed. His right arm maneuvered the shooter's head in a half-Nelson, although not as tight as he wanted, but one he had done repeatedly with large crocodiles, while his left arm was responsible for two jobs: holding the knife and twisting the gunman's body so the spray of rapid-fire would be instantly redirected over the heads of Sahib and Elder Cadmar. The decision to execute the quick action included many risks, and the physical requirements included strength and agility, but above all, Mitch understood that once his feet made the decision to run at the gunman, his mind would have to follow. *Justification.* His Melantha blues had weighed the reasons for taking another human life, while hidden behind the hut with Abeba. He knew sleepless nights would accompany killing another man, but had decided it was the best choice. It wasn't an action he performed lightly, nor was it an act he took any type of pleasure in. It was clearly a choice. Either let Sahib and possibly Elder Cadmar die, or take out the threat. Mitch wasn't religious, but could still remember his best friend's family discussing the right to kill in warfare, a topic that came up after his friend had joined the Army following high school, and one that played out as his uniformed friend had taken leave from the United States Army after completing boot camp. Mitch recalled the topic being bounced around like a beach ball, while Chase's family grilled steaks and drank beer in celebration of Chase's accomplishment. *God ordered people to kill aggressors in warfare.* He recalled Chase's step-dad reciting. *It's in Genesis.* Mitch had listened to his friend's family talk about how God-sanctioned warfare; he tried to rationalize what was happening in front of him. *Was it an act of warfare?* He knew the gunman would kill Sahib before returning to his village with the cattle he had recaptured, and Elder Cadmar's community would be targeted whenever the young soldier felt compelled to do so. The sleepy village would become victimized over and over again. There was no alternative. Sahib had fucked up, but it was clear that simply retrieving the cattle wasn't enough for the two young intruders.

Mitch should have exercised his right to kill the gunman while he had his body positioned in the stronghold, but the young intruder wiggled his way free and had somehow managed to turn the Ak-47 toward Mitch. Sahib knew the entire situation was his fault, and he knew Mitch's life was now at stake. Jumping between Mitch and the gun, he felt the warmth from the gun's barrel through his shirt, one that had been warmed after emptying one magazine and nearly emptying a second, and one that would finish its job – now. Sahib's young body had wedged itself between Mitch and the man with the repositioned Ak-47.

"I love you." Those were the last three words Sahib got out before the gunman squeezed the angled trigger. Spray. Empty. *Dry firing.* The snapping sound quickly processed inside Mitch's conscious mind, as did Sahib's words – *I love you.* Mitch knew the words were meant for him, words that were meant to be the last ever spoken by Sahib, after he had made the quick decision to step between the gunman and the white father figure that he needed so badly.

Feeling even more empowered, Mitch's actions were swift. First, he knocked Sahib out of the way. Then he grabbed the muscular build from behind, once again, this time placing him into a half-Nelson that was unwavering, before spinning his own body in the dirt, a dance move that placed the gunman's face on the opposite side of the camp, blocking Sahib's view of the knife that went deep and hard inside the gunman's throat. It was over within seconds, leaving the second tribesman in complete shock. Unarmed he took off on foot. Mitch released the dead gunman's body, letting it fall to the earth before he took off running after the second intruder. *Unarmed.* It was a detail that made Mitch question his mission. *I wonder what God would say about this.* Unaddressed, he ran – hard.

Sahib realized the severity of his actions and chased after Mitch to stop further bloodshed. He didn't understand that the two men were from a tribe where retaliation would be constant and unforgiving.

"Mitch." He yelled his name, as he weaved through cattle that were roped and waiting. There wasn't an answer, nor did Mitch slow. He stopped for breath, after failing to keep up with Mitch, who he now knew could run faster than the cheetah in his childhood village.

It seemed like an hour passed before Mitch worked his way back to the tiny village, that was still in fear. The day had started with the sound of rapid gunfire, noise that had woken an otherwise quiet village. Now, a dead youth was laying at the feet of Elder

Cadmar and six cattle that he knew didn't belong to his village stood under African juniper trees, where Sahib was sitting in tears, after failing to catch up with Mitch.

"Dammit Sahib." Mitch's voice was firm and deliberately aimed at Sahib's tearful face. "You fucking know better."

"I'm sorry Mitch." The words came out as Sahib heaved a sigh. "I don't want you killed."

"Your actions made me kill Sahib." It was a strong but accurate statement. "I can't fix what I had to do to protect you and this village."

Sahib hadn't thought about the repercussions when he took the cattle in the middle of the night, but now, in the light of day, as he stared at the visible blood splatter on Mitch's clothing, he knew his plan to marry Abeba hadn't been well thought out.

Elder Cadmar approached the two of them, while everyone else in the village seemed to stay hidden, expect for Abeba who was at her father's side.

"Kill wrong." Mitch listened to the elder's broken English, as he imagined what was coming next. *Banishment.* Mitch waited for their dismissal, knowing it was well deserved. "Save good." It was a slight contradiction, so Mitch stood quietly, allowing the elder to finish whatever he wanted to say. "Thank you."

"I'm sorry I killed the gunman," Mitch spoke slowly wanting the elder to understand his words. "I had to protect Sahib." He looked into the elder's eyes. "My son." He felt Sahib's small hand take his.

"Brave like father." Elder Cadmar looked into Sahib's eyes. It was a look that said he understood the young boy's actions. "You marry my daughter Abeba." He smiled at Sahib, who was trying to figure out if Elder Cadmar had just given him his blessing.

"I love Abeba." Sahib made sure his face was absent of tears before speaking to the elder. "Please let her be my wife." It was a slow and deliberate request.

"Yes." It was one word, but it touched the lives of many. Mitch knew that Elder Cadmar wasn't banishing them from the village. Sahib knew that the angel in front of him would become his wife, and Abeba's eyes glistened as she smiled at Sahib.

Sometimes extreme actions are called for, and the sins of mankind will avoid judgment. It was a day when everyone in the village was reminded of that. Now, after the elder's signal, a movement where he thrust both arms up over his head, fists closed tightly, everyone in hiding came forward. Without instruction, several women carried the body of the gunman away to an area just outside the small village, where two male members of the community were already digging a deep grave. It would remain unmarked, and prayers would be optional and private. Two other men, both around Mitch's age started repairs on Elder Cadmar's hut. Others picked up shell casings. And, two elderly women walked up to Sahib and Mitch to exchange hugs. By sunset, everyone in the village, at one time or another, had stopped to shake the hand of Sahib and Mitch.

"I love you too." Mitch looked over at Sahib as he spoke, bringing the young boy to a sudden halt. He turned briefly, long enough to smile at the white man who had saved him, before he continued to guide the cattle into the corn maze behind Cadmar's hut, an area where they would be out of sight from a possible passerby, and an area where they would be slaughtered as needed to feed the community. Each bite would go down easy. There wouldn't be a member who found the stolen cattle unworthy. They were a blessing, a gift, and would be treated as such. "When you're done placing the cattle, come with me." Sahib was still sneaking looks in Mitch's direction, and he was still allowing Mitch's words of admiration to sink in. "It's time for you to be a man."

Mitch led Sahib a good forty or fifty minutes into the thick jungle that separated Ethiopia from Kenya. He stopped when he came upon the lifeless body of the second youth, the one that had begged for his life in a language Mitch didn't understand.

"Dig." He handed Sahib his knife, the blade still painted a dark red. "He needs a grave Sahib."

Sahib got down on his knees. Alone. Making a large outline in the soil with the same blade that had taken the man's life, he chiseled and scooped up handfuls of earth. Mitch sat near Sahib, silently at first, giving him time to think about the consequences that had followed his decision. Over an hour passed before Sahib had cleared enough dirt to accommodate the body.

"Will you help me put him in there?" Sahib asked Mitch.

"No, you need to do it." He moved aside allowing Sahib to get close to the dead man's head, where he watched him lock his eight-year-old arms, one under each arm of the dead man. Dragging him, at times with every ounce of strength, he gently rolled the dark-skinned body into the grave.

"Should I pray for him before covering him up?" Sahib asked through tears, trying not to look at the young man's bloody neck, one that had been cut straight across.

"It's up to you if you pray or not Sahib." Then before Sahib could react. "I want you to look at his face," Mitch said forcefully. "That's what war looks like." His statement was meant to make Sahib think. "That's death."

"I am sorry Mitch." He said it again. This time without crying. "Will he be reborn?" He asked, then after remembering the word Mitch had used at the bonfire, "reincarnated?"

"I don't know Sahib." Then he tried to answer, as he took into consideration what he hoped was true. "I would like to believe he will be." He paused. "Maybe he will come back a better son." It was a strange choice of words; Mitch knew he was judging himself. *It's too late.* It was a short thought, and one he questioned the validity of. *Is it too late to be a good son?* He silently questioned as he watched Sahib cover the man's body with soil, and he silently got his answer as he listened to Sahib pray over the dead man's body:

"You make bad decision. It cost life." Sahib struggled to keep his voice from wavering. "I make decision that almost cost me life." He thought about how he had taken the cattle. "If you get reborn," then after searching his mind for the unfamiliar word once again, "reincarnated," he corrected, "make love not war." He thought about his mother Maryam and how she always fought for family and love over everything else in life. "Be a good son," he added before ending his prayer. "Amen."

With dry eyes, he covered the man's body with soil.

CHAPTER THIRTY-FIVE

ALASKA

Enola had learned about the first quake that rocked the Aleut Islands when she stopped in Coldfoot, in the middle of her slow and easy process of descending the Dalton. She imagined a lot of the road damage that she encountered on her trip down the Dalton was caused by the 7.2 quake. And, although she hadn't heard anyone state the obvious, she wondered if that's why animals were herding east, away from the danger. She also wondered if that's why her cell phone didn't work in places it had on the way up. *Maybe it even caused that portion of the pipeline to become unstable.* She thought, remembering the explosion that had knocked her flat. *I'm sure the quake affected the commercial truck transportation too.* There were things she wasn't wondering about, like the coast of Oregon, or the northeast section of Africa. She wasn't wondering because she didn't know about the other quakes, and she certainly hadn't heard about the Aleutian Island quake sending a tsunami to the Oregon coast.

She was unknowingly fortunate, driving in an area where regular gasoline wasn't the shortage. Diesel fuel was the shortage near the Dalton Highway travel; regular gasoline was plentiful in that area. Filling up her tank in Coldfoot was enough to get her off the Dalton, and after topping her tank off at the self-service pump in front of the Yukon Camp, she had enough gas for the next 300 plus miles.

Gasoline wasn't the issue; being emotionally drained was the problem. Spotting the familiar parking lot, the same one she had turned around in ten days earlier, she slowly pulled in. Her plan was simple. First, she would heat water for a Cup-a-Soup, then she would grab a short nap, only a few hours, before making her way on Alaska

Highway 2. *Two hours tops*, she calculated. It was a safe estimation, one that allowed her to make the outskirts of Fairbanks before dark.

Enola was startled after, first, noticing the night sky, a sign that she had exceeded her two-hour nap, and second, after feeling her car move, as if someone was pushing it. She attempted to sit upright, but her mind held her body captive, as she questioned the sanctuary of the small parking lot. *Was someone trying to tow my vehicle?* Maybe she had misread the generosity of Hubcap Harry's, a mom-and-pop business that appeared to welcome an occasional guest in their parking lot, at the end of a cul-de-sac, a safety-net after surviving the Dalton. *Maybe I should have asked?* She privately questioned the darkness that surrounded her, before realizing the darkness didn't include the flashing lights of a tow truck. *No one is near my Jeep.* She answered her last two questions.

Pushing her body into a sitting position, she pulled up the window screen she often used at night, giving herself a clear view of the world outside. Her last thought was correct; there wasn't anyone around. No people. No tow-truck. Not even a territorial moose, who was pushing her away from his personal space.

"Another one?" It was a question she asked out loud, and the only one that made logical sense to her. In the back of her darkened Jeep, she studied Miles' face, which fought the golden selenite crystal for position to Enola's upper thigh. Miles seemed unable to move out of fear, conceding to the Brazilian crystal. She rubbed her co-pilot's head in the darkness, hoping the shaking would stop, both for him and the world around her. It did. Finally.

Enola was able to coax Miles into movement so that she could bend her legs at both knees to accommodate the rear passenger door's opening, while her right hand reached for the inside door lever, and her left hand grabbed the healing crystal, tucking it into her jean pocket, before she opened the door slowly, unsure of what she would see first. Her eyes focused on a man and woman standing in front of Hubcap Harry's near the rear of the lot. Their bodies almost blended into the night sky. Clipping Miles to his leash, using the same hand that had hidden the Brazilian crystal deep inside her front jean pocket, she persuaded him to leave the vehicle, and together they slowly walked toward the couple, that even in the dark she could tell were advanced in years.

"Anchorage area again," the elderly man said.

"I hope everyone's okay," the woman followed up, then acknowledged Enola with a smile as she got closer, before becoming fixated on the pup that seemed to cautiously walk on the earth's surface. "Poor baby, he's scared to death." The gray-haired woman carefully extended her hand to pet Miles' head, cautiously aware of her balance. "You okay, baby?" Like Enola often did with Miles, she waited for an answer. He licked the woman's hand, thanking her for the extra attention.

"I'm not used to earthquakes," Enola stated to the woman. "Neither is he." She was referring to Miles, who still had the woman's attention.

"I'm pretty certain that was a volcanic eruption." The man that had seen at least eighty years stated. "Definitely." The man rubbed his arm, removing a light layer of gritty ash. It wasn't until Enola looked at the man's open hand, a blackened shadow, under the dim moonlight, that she realized it was raining ash all around them.

"Volcano." The woman looked at her husband, as she dusted gray soot off her arms, and turned to face the old wooden building,

whose white letters – H-u-b-c-a-p-H-a-r-r-y-s – were darkening.
"Come on everyone," she ordered. "Bring that cute puppy." Miles
was already pulling toward the shop front, to no avail, because
Enola's feet stayed glued in place, until Harry slipped his ash-
covered arm up under her left, and set her into motion.

"Let's go," Harry ordered. They reached the front door of the
shop, just as Sarah was wetting towels, and urging them to shut the
door. Quickly.

"Roll these up into draft stoppers." Sarah handed Enola
several wet towels, which she quickly rolled into log shapes, after
letting go of Miles' leash. "Then give them to Harry." Quickly,
Enola did as she was told to do. All the while, her mind worked to
piece together the ashy tracks that had followed them inside,
stopping when they hit a large area rug. One set of ashy bedroom
slipper prints, plus one set of ashy paw prints, plus one set of ashy
boot prints, plus one set of ashy sneaker prints, combined with a
residue that seemed to cover Enola's arm tattoo and Miles' white
and golden-yellow fur, equals one volcanic eruption.

Enola's head was spinning as she tried to wrap her mind around what was happening, then before she could organize her thoughts the world began to shake again, but this time it was much stronger. It seemed to last forever. A ceramic coffee cup hit the floor near a small table. Miles was struggling to get underneath one of its matching chairs.

"We've never had one that lasted that long," the woman stated, as she fought to pull Miles up into her arms.

"It was almost five minutes long." The man announced.

"Was that an earthquake?" Enola asked the elderly man's darkened silhouette.

"Yes, and the longer the time, the stronger the magnitude." He informed Enola. "That was a big one." He concluded.

Several small aftershocks continued to poke at Anchorage, and even as far away as Livengood, taking the electricity out, but only for a few minutes, then Harry's pride and joy, a Cummins Quiet Connect generator, popped on, lighting up the inside of the small mom and pop business, along with Harry's set of bushy eyebrows and accompanying set of squinty blue eyes.

"A volcano erupted and then there was an earthquake?" She asked the question, as she handed the rolled wet towels off to Harry, who quickly placed one at the front door's threshold and one at the base of each window, before he took a seat in front of an old roll-top desk, where Miles had finally found refuge under its large oak base, after Sarah had gently sat him down to get his bearings, while she continued to pass out wet rolled towels, enough to block outside air from entering under window seals and doors. Enola placed the last one at the end of a small picture window near the front door, before listening to Harry speak.

"Breaker, breaker, this is Hubcap Harry, reaching out to Slim Jim." Enola watched his finger release a black button, as she freed Miles from his hiding spot, and gently pulled him into her arms. Sarah was standing behind her when she turned around, holding two more wet towels: one for Miles and one for the ashy face that wanted answers.

"Yes, it was a volcano then a quake," Sarah answered Enola's question, one Enola wasn't even sure she had asked out loud, before she poured two cups of black coffee, and motioned Enola to a wicker-backed chair in a small seating area behind the counter. For a moment, Enola thought of Homer and Barbara Parrish's porch in Florida, her grandparents that died many years ago. She felt comfortable, and was searching for words to express her gratitude, but under the circumstances her vocabulary was limited.

"Thanks, Sarah," Enola said. Simple. "This is Miles." Enola gently wiped his fur, removing ash particles that had discolored him. "And, I'm Enola." She extended her right hand.

"Harry will find out what's going on." She answered the worry in her face, after shaking Enola's hand. "Don't fret." She insisted. "You'll be safe here." Enola didn't doubt the woman's reassurance. "But, if you don't mind my asking, what are you doing way up here alone?" Sarah's curious tone revealed that she had taken notice of Enola's Washington plates.

"Alaska was on my bucket list." Enola smiled. "My forty-ninth state." Trying to find the humor in the last ten days of her travels, especially the last six days, she continued. "I made it all the way to Deadhorse, but had a really hard time getting back." Her mind calculated how many times she had come close to death on Dalton's Highway. *Dangerous road conditions. Explosion. Downed tree. Fire. Hazardous air alert.* Not to mention all the animals that had simply passed in front of her moving vehicle.

"I'm glad you made it back down the Dalton." She looked at Enola. "Several truckers tried to make it north after the first quake, but had to turn around because of fuel shortage and road damage." Enola wondered if Sarah knew about the explosions, the fires, the road obstructions, and the bizarre behavior of the animals. For a moment she considered talking about it but was distracted by Harry's voice.

"Key up for five more, and tell me your situation." Enola could hear the concern in Harry's voice, so did Sarah.

"Probably Mount Spurr." She looked at Enola. "Nothing has been reported in the news, but I felt its restlessness." Sarah paused thinking about the vision she had a few nights back, one where her dead son told her that Spurr was shaking again, but she didn't want to spook Enola by disclosing her ability to see and hear ghosts.

"Mount Spurr?" Enola asked, recalling that she had stood in awe, studying the overwhelming stature of Mount Spurr that could be seen from Anchorage, a breathtaking view, just across Cook Inlet, one she had snapped several photos of, before heading to Fairbanks, and before making her way up the Dalton.

"I always believed an earthquake could wake up Mount Spurr." She stated.

Enola took a long sip of black coffee, letting it warm her, while Miles dozed off, his head in her lap, as she listened to Sarah talk about the 1992 eruption of Mount Spurr. She talked about how it had taken the life of her only son, a volcanologist.

"Eddie loved walking the outer rim, collecting rock samples to prove his theories." Sarah smiled with tears in her eyes.

"Eddie was your son?" Enola questioned.

"Yes, and my Eddie loved his career." She stated. "He was convinced that Mount Spurr was a trigger, just waiting for an earthquake that wanted to be the bullet." She looked at Enola. "He'd be in his late fifties if he were still alive." She wiped several tears away. "He died doing what he loved." Emotion tried to tangle her words. "He fell to his death during the last eruption."

"I'm sorry Sarah." Enola's eyes matched hers, as the space around them bled melancholy, and as the ground around them seemed to roll underneath their feet, a movement Enola associated with the simultaneous scooting of Harry's desk chair, after he backed it across the oak flooring, but one that seemed to become stronger underneath the small wooden structure, sucking the life out of the earth. Harry didn't move for a moment, and sat in the chair that had held him during his conversation with Slim Jim in complete silence, before his body stood, walking away from the roll-top desk, and making its way to the sitting area, where an empty seat waited. Enola watched Harry's weathered hand take Sarah's hand, giving it a slight squeeze.

"I just lost contact." His face said a lot more; it said he suspected the reason their communication had come to an abrupt end.

"Usually the CB Radios hold-up well," Sarah replied, then catching herself, she put it together. *Rolling motion. Loss of contact.* Her face said she knew something she wasn't saying.

"What?" Enola asked.

"Tsunami." Harry's answer was only one word.

Sarah clenched her elderly husband's hand. "Jim is a fighter," she said. Enola listened to the unspoken sadness that was exchanging before her.

Eruption. Earthquake. And now, *tsunami?* Enola questioned herself privately, before going back to being an observer.

"They've got ash and rock everywhere. Jim said it looked like a war zone, but needed more light to tell the extent of the damage." Harry wiped a tear that was working down the front of his face, as he thought of his lifelong friend, a man who had saved his life in the Cold War, pulling him to safety in a Korean battlefield in 1952, sixty-seven years ago, just seconds before a grenade blew their foxhole all to hell. "Crazy fool even went outside in the middle of the quake, after figuring out the high-pitched squeal outside was his flag pole toppling over." He tried to chuckle, while his mind tried to convince his instincts that a tsunami hadn't just hit Anchorage. "He said the damn thing sounded like a poorly played violin." He took a sip of coffee that Sarah had handed to him. "Mother nature had to use some pretty strong hands to get that flag pole to bend."

Sarah pulled her hand away, then put her arm around her husband of sixty-nine years, as she pictured Jim's eighty-seven-year-old body, the same age as Harry, scrambling out after a volcanic eruption and during a quake to save an American Flag from ruin, as it lay in a pool of ash and debris. Harry poured out more details as if reading from a script, an attempt to get his mind off events that he was sure had followed the quake.

"Jim said it was stronger than the '64 quake." Harry's emotions could no longer be contained. Enola sat still watching the most painful thing she had ever seen – tears from an eighty-five-year-old man. "Jimmy said his CB radio had been blowing up with shout-outs from nearly everywhere in Alaska, two from the Yukon, David from British Columbia, Ernie down in Washington State, and even Troy in north Oregon."

Sarah was holding both of her hands to her face, as she imagined every glass window and door in Anchorage in pieces. She knew there were buildings reduced to remnants, even some that had been built to withstand a major earthquake.

"I knew the 7.2 was an opening act," she said, "but I didn't think anything would every top Prince William's quake." She was referring to the location of the 1964 Alaskan quake's epicenter – Prince William Sound – before recalling the tsunami that followed it. "You know that one sent tsunami waves racing 600 mph down the coast, hitting Crescent City, California and Oregon's coast." Then to ease Harry's mind, "I don't think a tsunami is going to hit near the quake's epicenter."

Enola held Miles tighter, as she listened to history and wisdom unfold in front of her, and as her thoughts went to Allie. *Is she okay?* Enola wondered. *Is she in danger?* She would give anything to hear her daughter's voice, and even more if she could hear Mitch's too. Fighting back tears, she listened to Harry and Sarah Locklear talk about life, raising babies, being faithful and kind, and enjoying life's simple pleasures – family being at the top of the list. It was a conversation where emotions ran high for Enola, and being an active listener was the best she could do.

By time the clock inside Hubcap Harry's revealed the time of 6:32, Enola had guzzled down a second cup of black coffee, had eaten a piece of toast with two strips of bacon, and had witnessed Miles talk Sarah into a scrambled egg with his puppy dog eyes. Harry took his usual – black coffee, one egg over-easy, and two strips of bacon. No toast.

"Thank God for generators," Harry announced, making sure his generator got credit, as he showed his appreciation for early morning breakfast. Then smiling at his lifelong mate, he became more serious. "Thank God for my Sarah." He announced passionately.

"I can't thank the two of you enough." Enola followed suit, addressing both of them after Sarah sat down with her plate – one slice of wheat toast with butter and strawberry jam. No egg. No bacon. "But I have to keep moving." Enola continued. "My daughter is probably worried like crazy." Encla formed what she had been wanting to say. "I'm really worried about her."

Harry pushed himself away from the table, minutes later returning with a red and black satellite phone. "Use this before you go." He handed the phone to Enola. "You'll need to step outside to make the call." He smiled. "Just point the antenna up at the sky, then dial 00, plus 1, plus the area code, plus your daughter's number before you leave." Enola stood, hugging the man whose squinty blues had shown her so much kindness, then hurried outside to call Allie.

Ten minutes later she was on 2 East.

CHAPTER THIRTY-SIX

CANADA

"We have to find a way to cross the Canadian border." Allie's tone was demanding.

The sky was closing in on the twenty-sixth of August, and with every ounce of daylight that disappeared the world felt colder. Reese and Allie were back in their vehicle, after talking to the border patrol officer inside the Sumas building, and after learning about the destruction caused by the severe quake; it had damaged roadways, throughout Alaska, and into British Columbia. A series of words continuously cycled in Allie's mind, as she tried to formulate a plan. *Eruption. Mudslides. Ash. Danger. Mom.*

"Allie, there's no way to sneak across the border. They have sensors to detect people trying to cross on foot." He knew what she was thinking, and he knew the Canadian border had started using Passive Infrared Sensor Systems, just like the ones they used along the Mexican border, at least according to Reese's uncle in Vegas, who had spent his life helping design sensors that sent out signals after detection and had filled Reese's head with hours of talk about the PIR control systems. "Besides, we can't trek off into the Canadian wilderness with three dogs and a cat." He could tell by the way her eyes moved, that she wasn't thinking logically, and he knew the one-sided conversation needed to continue, so that she would hear parts of it. "Allie, your mom is still in Alaska, by this point." He watched her face process some of what he was saying. "She is at least two thousand miles away from us." He imagined that even if Enola had reached Tok, Alaska, the area where he knew she would stop to ship her firearm back to the lower forty-eight, she was still over 1800 miles away, on a good day.

"You're right." Her words were not expected, almost startling Reese.

"I'm sorry Allie." He knew she was at a breaking point. "We have enough food and gasoline to hang out in this area for another five days." He imagined Allie's mom would make Washington's border by then. "We'll wait for her." It was the only logical thing they could do, still, Allie felt uneasy, and wanted to at least hear her mother's voice. "We are close enough to the border patrol office so that we can check in every day for updates on conditions." It was an idea he thought might calm her.

"Okay." She didn't have anything else to say at the moment; instead, she drove without speaking back to the Sumas RV Park, where they could grab another cold shower and check to see if the office had opened. No one. It still had the appearance of a ghost town. In the light of day, Allie could see two fifth wheels parked in distant corners. Allie drove slowly by the first one before settling on

a new place to park. The first, a Jayco, sat uncovered on a small
gravel corner camp spot. Stabilizer jacks held the front-end sturdy.
Allie noticed that the nearby electrical receptacle stood empty, not
that there was electricity at the moment, but she wondered if it was a
sign that the owners had disconnected their vehicle and left.
Stopping in front of it, she looked at Reese. "I think we should
knock on the door and listen for movement," she suggested. Reese
knew the people were most likely gone, but still knocking on
someone's door could result in anything, especially during a natural
disaster, one where working cell towers, functional landlines, and
available gasoline had become nonexistent; still, talking Allie down
from whatever she was thinking had reached the limit for the day, so
he agreed.

"I'll do it," he said, then reached for the Tahoe's inside door
lever.

"Be careful." She was thinking about the last time he
approached someone's residence, so she retrieved the loaded P22
from the center console, keeping it within easy reach. She would
replay the scene they had encountered off Tree Farm Court if

needed, the one that involved old lady Margaret and her sexual predator adult son, a piece of shit she still regretted letting live. "I've got you covered." He looked back at her, his eyes expecting to make contact with the gun, which they did.

Several minutes later Reese returned to the Tahoe, one that waited with the camper, and one that held his life. "No movement inside." He was certain.

Allie swung around the other corner of the park, and into the next loop, this one a hard right from the Sumas RV Park office. It was a Keystone Montana, probably five or six years old. Reese and Allie both noticed two slide outs were in place, one directly in the center, possibly part of the kitchen, and a second slide out near the back, probably accommodating an extra bed.

"I think we should check this one out also." Allie had stopped directly in front of the Keystone. Reese, once again, made his way to the front. This time he heard a dog inside, a low almost muzzled growl came from its belly. *Restrained,* Reese thought, before turning around, making eye contact with Allie, and signaling that he had heard sound, first by touching his ear, then pointing toward the RV door. Allie picked up the P22, placing it on her lap.

Reese knocked on the door, then stood back. He could hear the shuffle of feet inside. *Human.* Again, he signaled Allie, this time by using the pointer and middle finger on his right hand as miniature legs and moving them back and forth while holding his hand in a downward position. Allie exited the vehicle, leaving the door open for the dogs that waited.

"Hello, would you please come to the door?" Reese asked, his tone was both loud and polite, but his question was only answered with gentle sobs. It sounded like a young girl. Maybe twelve or thirteen. He flagged Allie over. Cautiously, she approached and listened to Reese as he whispered. "A young girl is inside Allie." He felt certain. "And a dog."

"Yes, and maybe an adult or two, with guns." She whispered back.

"I don't think so," he said. "I think she's alone." Something told him he was right. Maybe it was the way she moved when he first knocked, or maybe it was the way he suspected the dog was staying near her, protecting her every move, a feeling the weighed heavily after he heard blubbering and a low growl coming from the same area behind the left side of the door. Whatever it was, Reese knew they couldn't walk away. Allie read him just as well as he read her, and without more words between them, she knew Reese wanted *her* to talk the child into opening the door.

"Sweetie, it's me Allie." She spoke loudly to the door. "Is your mom home?" It was a question that was answered with more tears, and a steady whimper that Allie could hear through the door. "Please open the door so I can help you." She handed the loaded P22 to Reese and watched him tuck it in the back of his waistband. There was no need to frighten a young child, and by now, both Allie and Reese were certain that was what they were dealing with. "I will help you." Then, hoping to at least get a response. "What is your name?" Allie sensed the hidden figure had moved more toward the door, a suspicion that was verified after both Allie and Reese could hear the whisper on the other side of the door.

"I'm Hope." Allie's face froze, thinking of the one word her mother had used repeatedly during the last couple of years, and the one thing her mother never lost sight of – hope. Now, Allie was listening to *it* on the other side of a closed door.

"Hi Hope. It sounds like your doggy is with you." Allie could talk about dogs all day and imagined the voice on the other side of the door was just as attached to her furry friend as Allie was to hers.

"His name is Buttons," Hope spoke without whispering.

"What a cute name," Allie said. "I have a Zeus, Shiloh, Yoda, and even a cat named Serenity."

"You do?" A slight sniffle followed.

"Yes, and if it's okay with your mom, I'd like you to meet them."

"My mom can't talk." The whimper grew into a persistent whine.

"Why?" Allie asked.

"She's dead." It was a statement that stopped Allie's heartbeat, if only for a few seconds.

"Are you alone?" Allie figured she was.

"No, I have Buttons and my mom."

Reese's eyed widened as he imagined the child's mother inside and unresponsive. Allie's thoughts were matching his.

"I need you to open the door, so we can look at your mother," she waited, before adding, "to see if she can be helped."

Reese backed away from the door another three or four feet, giving Allie room, in an attempt to make sure Hope didn't get spooked, after hearing the deadbolt click, as a result of being placed in an upright position, and watching the doorknob turn. Slowly.

When the door opened, Allie came face to face with a yellow lab and a young girl, no older than seven. The smell of death filled the inside of the RV. Allie motioned Hope and Buttons to come outside, and led them toward the Tahoe, where Shiloh, Zeus, and Yoda were on their best behavior. Animals know. They know good and evil. Shiloh came forward, sitting in front of Hope, and quickly swiped her long tongue on the girl's cheek. Allie reached for Serenity who had been sunbathing on the dashboard once again, and handed her to Hope.

"She's so soft." Hope held the black and white tuxedo cat tightly.

"Yes," Allie stated, then saw Reese exiting the RV. His head was shaking side to side, with one hand over his mouth, and the other holding what looked like a phone.

"Hope needs to come with us." He said, still trying to shake the smell of dead flesh. "Rigor mortis." It was the only adult way he knew to inform Allie that Hope's mother was dead, an obvious overdose, probably unintentional, but one having the same outcome for Hope. An empty pill bottle and empty whiskey bottle were near the dead woman, details he quietly and discreetly shared with Allie before he went back inside to make sure that he grabbed any usable food from the refrigerator, one that he noticed had been working off the built-in generator, and one that had kept seven-year-old Hope stocked with some basic food – milk, cheese, bologna, and part of an apple that he saw on the bottom shelf.

"What the fuck?" Allie quietly stated her question when Reese came back outside while trying to process how a mother could do that to her child.

"It's fucked up Allie." He answered the question she had whispered, while one of his hands grasped a full bag of usable groceries, and his other passed Allie the Iridium satellite phone he had been holding. "We can try to get in touch with your mother." He smiled. "Or at least figure out how to check your cell's voicemail to see if she left a message."

Allie nodded. She would see if her own mother had left her a message as soon as she sorted out the inadvertent message left by Hope's mother – *You're not as important as my drugs.*

An hour passed before Allie listened to her voicemail, first, she watched Reese cook dinner for Hope – a hot plate of macaroni and cheese with a hot dog – then, she watched him feed four dogs and a cat before she called Whatcom County Police Department with the satellite phone to report the overdose and Hope's whereabouts, and before trying to dial her own mother's cell. No answer. Following disappointment, she figured out how to check her cell phone messages using the satellite phone – by dialing her cell number with a one and pushing star

Hope's laughter filled the small camper, so did the message from Allie's mother. Allie played it over and over.

CHAPTER THIRTY-SEVEN

ETHIOPIA

Several men in the small Ethiopian village banged lightly on kebero drums, their hands rhythmically tapping the animal hide stretched over both ends of the double-headed drum. Mitch and Sahib stood watching them. The vibration of cowhide over the hollowed-out section of an irókò tree could be heard throughout the village. Mitch whispered to Sahib as they stood facing the drummers.

"I'm happy for you Sahib."

"I will make you proud." He said. "I will be a good husband to Abeba."

"I know." Mitch looked at Sahib. He saw an eight-year-old boy, who lost both parents. Mitch knew the feelings associated with loss. He had been eight years old when his great-grandmother died, his father's grandmother and the only grandparent he knew as a child since his mother's family had dwindled down to nothing. He thought about his great-grandmother's death. It was expected for her age but came at a bad time in his childhood. Turning eight years old was the beginning of his world falling apart. It was also the same time period that his father, Rex Narducci, moved out, leaving him and his sister alone with Enola. He watched his mother balance a full-time job, homework, laundry, cooking, yard maintenance, years of Allie's ballet and cheerleading, his football and soccer, pets, tears, school activities, and somehow always keep her sanity.

The combination of soulful drum music matched the well-displayed setting – one where several baskets constructed out of banana leaves and bamboo were sitting on the ground, the insides filled with gifts for the young bride and groom. The music and setting stirred up emotions in Mitch that he hadn't felt in a while.

"You are a good son." He said to Sahib, as he studied the arrangement of white lily petals and yellow eucalyptus flowers scattered from the spot where he stood, and stretched to the far end of the village, creating a shape that formed an obvious walkway. Everyone who lived in the village lined both sides on the flowered walkway and was clapping and bouncing up and down in song, waiting for the appearance of Abeba. Several elderly women in the village were focused on the young bride, applying each finishing touch with meticulous care. Dressed in the colors of a rainbow, Abeba signified a new beginning. She wore a silk scarf over her head imprinted with brightly colored flowers, which was securely held in place by the bright orange turban that topped it. Abeba's earlobes had been quickly pierced using a large needle to accommodate the long earrings that dangled from the freshly made holes, each displaying a bright white ostrich feather, which nearly touched her covered shoulders, a part of her that had been draped with a cranberry colored scarf. Only two inches of her mid-drift showed above her tiny waistline. The rest of her body had been gently wrapped with a floor-length silver sheet. Both wrists were adorned with multicolored beaded bracelets, and her neck had been embellished with an off-yellow assortment of what looked like Indian corn. She took her father's arm, walking slowly down the flower-petaled pathway. Her dark eyes locked on Sahib's, who waited in a white linen shirt and dark pants, both of which were nearly too big, but matched Mitch's, Sahib's father and best man. The only noticeable difference between Sahib and Mitch's attire was the addition of blood splatter on Sahib's forehead, just a small dot, but one that was a deep red.

Elder Cadmar didn't see the point on postponing the ceremony, and had started his day off early, first by officially accepting the dowry paid for Abeba from Sahib – six small cattle – then, by watching Sahib slaughter one of the cattle during the early morning, a ritual which after its completion, Elder Cadmar then blessed Sahib into manhood, a custom that included placing a dot of cow's blood on the young boy's forehead.

The sacrament had taken place during the early morning hours on the twenty-seventh, while most tribal members in the village slept, except for Mitch, who wanted to offer Sahib his support, first by letting him use his knife, and then by verbally instructing him on how to sacrifice the calf.

"Stand on the left side of the calf, Sahib," Mitch instructed. "Lean over him, and grab both of his legs near the ground on the calf's right side, flipping him to the ground." Mitch showed Sahib by demonstrating with his own hands on an imaginary cow. "You have to get him flat on the ground, son." Sahib understood and didn't waste time before leaning, grabbing, and pulling the small calf's legs upright. Mitch watched Sahib's eyes fight tears after a loud thump vibrated the ground, as a seventy-pound mound of brown and white curly fur hit solid earth. Sahib had used every ounce of strength he had to flip a calf that outweighed him.

"Is he hurt?" Mitch knew the answer to Sahib's question was unimportant but wanted to answer his son's compassionate question with a compassionate answer.

"Get down on your knees. Use one hand and arm to keep the calf down on his side, and use the other to stroke his head and neck area." He watched Sahib's shaky arms follow directions, and fought tears himself as he watched Sahib's left hand stroke the locks of curly white fur around the calf's neck. "Good." It was only one word but was full of empathy and understanding. "Don't make him suffer, Sahib. Cut across the entire neck. You must be quick. Cut deep and fast."

Sahib looked at Mitch, his eyes pleading for an alternate ritual, but he didn't want to show any sign of weakness in front of his new father or Elder Cadmar, who had been watching every movement. He pulled the knife from the leather sheath, where it had waited, less than a foot away from where he was kneeling. He cut fast and deep. Straight across. He watched the calf's eyes dim as the earth soaked up red gore.

"You man." Elder Cadmar spoke the words after kneeling near the bloodshed, where he fingered the young calf's throat, absorbing then applying a fingertip amount of the animal's blood to his future son-in-law's forehead.

That moment was an emotional flashback for Mitch, one where he thought about his own life in the states. Eight-year-old Sahib's blessing for marriage reminded Mitch of his own mother's marriage, one where he participated at age ten, and one where he watched his step-father display the same nervous grin. Those tender thoughts chilled him in the early morning as he thought of his mother, 8000 miles away, and eleven hours behind. He wondered what she was doing, and tried to imagine her routine on a Monday, the last one in August. His lack of knowledge saddened him, especially when he realized he knew nothing about her life anymore. *Was she sitting in an apartment in Washington State watching her favorite television show?* He wondered. *Was she in a happy relationship with a new man? Did Allie talk to her almost every day?* He didn't have any answers for the questions that plagued him, as he watched Sahib's rite of passage, or even later when he watched Abeba approaching, locked arm and arm with her father, while he and Sahib waited at the end of the flowery walkway.

Mitch watched Sahib clutch Abeba's hand after it was placed in his own by Elder Cadmar. It was decorated with henna, both on her palms and fingernails. Turning to face the villagers, the elder placed himself on the far side of the young couple. Mitch wondered if he should have helped Sahib write vows. *Shit.* His thought was that of a nervous dad but was quickly relieved when he sensed the young couple would be silently participating. They did not recite vows; instead, they listened to the words of Elder Cadmar. Mitch wished he could understand Oromo, but knew the tone was serious and watched Sahib shake his head in agreeance after words like *hinsoban, dhirsa, niitii,* and *onnee.* Sahib's admiring eyes could see Mitch's confusion and whispered the English translation to his father.

"Don't cheat. Husband. Wife. Love with heart." Mitch smiled at Sahib, thanking him.

"Nigammadani." Elder Cadmar looked at his son-in-law and daughter.

"They became happy," Sahib whispered to Mitch while smiling at his bride.

"Baga gammadde." It was the last thing said by Elder Cadmar before he hugged his daughter and shook the hand of Sahib.

"Congratulations." Sahib translated for Mitch, then turned to kiss his bride slowly and with great apprehension. It was his first kiss but left him wanting more.

Mitch stood by, giving his son time to enjoy the awkward pleasure before he reached to pull Sahib in for a hug.

"Congratulations." He repeated back to him, and then with a flare of educated eloquence, he pulled Abeba close, first to give her a hug, then to speak loudly, so that the elder and villagers, who were listening to every word, could hear. "Baga gammadde." Abeba smiled, knowing it took effort to remember how to say congratulations in Oromo. It was a gesture that sent everyone in the village into song once again, and like well-rehearsed dancers on stage, they moved in unison, each villager giving the new bride and groom room to walk the flowered path, one that led south to the couple's newly constructed hut, that had been worked on throughout the day by villagers. Several women carried the baskets of fruit behind the couple: a colorful arrangement of mango, pineapple, bananas, and papaya in each.

Watching Sahib and Abeba walk into their new life, he thought of his mother once again. More questions followed. *Was his mother happy? Had his sister Allie gotten married?* A part of him thought it was time to travel back to the United States, even if it was only long enough to see his mother and sister. He knew, from talking to various boat captains off the coast of Somalia, that Djibouti was located just north of Ethiopia, probably two or three days by foot, and had numerous military bases in the small country, one of which was a large American military base – Camp Lemonnier. He also knew it was a place where he could get assistance with transportation back to the United States. Mitch thought about the freight liner he had worked for, thought about his merchant mariner's license that would still be on record for identification purposes, and thought about the man he had talked to at the U.S. Embassy nearly three years back, just before deciding to stay in Somalia. *Is it time?* His question was directed at the late Ethiopian sunset. He knew it would be a lot of paperwork, and possibly a wait, but it would allow his new son to become a man on his own merits. He would return.

That night, Mitch spoke to Elder Cadmar. He made sure the elder understood enough to explain his absence to Sahib. "I go. See mother. See sister. I return."

"Leave son?" Elder Cadmar asked.

"I come back."

"Yes."

"With summer rain." Mitch clarified.

"Maze tall?"

"Yes." Mitch agreed. And after feeling like the elder understood he added, "Leave sunlight."

"You safe."

"Yes." He shook the elder's hand, before retiring to his hut, where he slept until first light. Come morning, Mitch removed the Smith and Wesson knife from his boot, the same one that had killed crocodiles, the same one that had taken the lives of a gunman and his accomplice, the same one that had dug one intruder's grave, and the same one that had slaughtered a young calf. He placed it on Sahib's empty cot. It would be discovered hours later by Sahib, tucked inside its leather sheath with the words *My Son* carved into the leather casing. Beside it was Sahib's necklace – the bright green NY lanyard adorned with the abalone pendant. Goodbye wasn't in Mitch's vocabulary.

CHAPTER THIRTY-EIGHT

ALASKA

It was almost seven in the morning when Enola left Harry and Sarah.

Heavy rain followed her. *At least it's not more ash,* she thought. *The*

rain will wash some of this mess away. Carefully and slowly, she

made her way on Alaskan Highway 2 East, mostly because of the

weather, and partially because her body craved more sleep, so

driving with extra caution was a priority. Even though the nap she

started yesterday, after first cooking and eating soup, and before

walking Miles in the corner of Hubcap Harry's parking lot, had turned into seven hours instead of the two hours she had originally planned, she had been up since midnight, first experiencing the earth move because of a major volcanic eruption almost 400 miles away, topped with what Sarah categorized as a "very severe" earthquake, and even though it hadn't been verified by the time she left the Locklear's mom-and-pop business and home, she believed old man Harry's instincts were right. *A fucking tsunami.* It was a possibility that made hearing Allie's voice that much more urgent. She imagined Harry was probably right about the rolling motion felt hundreds of miles away, but the part she knew he would have no way of knowing, at least not yet, was where it hit. *Maybe the coast of Oregon,* she imagined, not knowing one had already devastated the small town of Seaside just five days earlier.

Paul Wabel knew the second tsunami off the Pacific coast didn't hit Oregon. It had annihilated Anchorage, its defenseless city already in ruins, and had filled Paul Wabel's lungs with salty ocean water. The cerebral cortex in the front part of Paul's brain knew his lungs were filling with blood, a hypertonic reaction to the salt intake. It took him almost fifteen minutes to drown in his own fluids, the last five of which his amygdala took over, allowing Paul to revert back to Paulie, and allowing his last thought to form from the neurons deep in his temporal lobe. *Mother was right about Sleeping Lady.*

Enola's strong maternal instincts were kicking in. She wished for cell service, knowing it would calm her nerves. Hearing Allie's voice would lift her spirits; although, Harry and Sarah Locklear had provided everything humanly possible: shelter during the volcanic eruption and earthquake, breakfast, comfort, conversation, information, and even the use of an old Garmin satellite phone that Harry selflessly pulled down from a back closet before Enola left, allowing Enola to reach out to Allie. No answer. It had been disappointing to not hear Allie's voice, but at least Enola was able to leave a voicemail on Allie's cell phone. *Maybe towers were knocked out up and down the coastline,* Enola rationalized. *After all, it didn't ring; it simply went to voicemail.* Enola's thoughts continued as she maneuvered the curvy mountainous road, recalling bits and pieces of the message she left for Allie. The message she left wasn't very long but seemed to cover feelings that stirred inside, feelings that had reached an all-time high during the last week when days were filled with doubts about her own survival.

Now, Enola was headed home, piloting her Jeep, that dripped with dust and ash, some of which writhed its way down the front windshield, creating squiggly patterns. Vertically shaped mountainside lined the left side of the road, offering protection against the high winds that had joined the steady rain.

Twenty-minutes into her drive, Enola eyed the pipeline on her right, a constant friend over the last ten days of her life. Pulling over just before Pump Station 7, she exited her Jeep in a large open area, where a high mountain of earth blocked the wind. The rain had slowed to a drizzle, offering the opportunity to test cellphone reception once again, let Miles pee, and put her emotions in order. After leashing Miles, she fingered the golden selenite which was hidden deep inside her left jean front pocket, mostly for comfort, but also for the glimmer she felt beckoned her grasp. She held Miles steady on his retractable leash with her right, and grasped the healing crystal in her left palm, as she let the untimed drops of rain hit her bare arms and face; all the while, allowing them to drip down her cheekbones without making the slightest effort to interrupt their flow. Rainwater beaded at the end of her chin, minus what had been held captive in her hair. Enola liked the rain. Every time it rained, Enola imagined the world was being cleansed and getting the chance to begin once again. *A new start,* she thought as she walked along the road.

Miles hated the rain, shaking off most of the unwanted liquid as they walked beside the base of the mountain. Enola looked back, making sure she had turned off her headlights. Her red Jeep Cherokee seemed to reciprocate her glance, with darkened lenses that looked like crying eyes in the late August shower. Each step, Enola could hear liquid squishing beneath her shoes. The sound made her giggle, as her eyes searched the end of the leash she was holding, an attempt to see if Miles' paws were experiencing the same mushy ground. She snickered again after realizing the gelatinous mud was sucking at each paw as he walked.

Stopping suddenly, he looked at her, his Detroit butterscotch eyes begged her to take action, as the sound of earth was being scraped up like a giant snow cone, the mixture rushing in their direction. Enola saw the concoction of mud and rock racing down the mountainside, pulling up trees from their roots, as her mind quickly calculated that it was moving at a speed which she couldn't outrun.

It's in those last moments when everything that's important plays like a movie. She felt Mitch's arm around her as they walked through the Little Rock Zoo. She heard Dixie tell her to keep moving. *Forward.* She saw Allie's face; it came close to hers, allowing the scent of coconut shampoo to fill her nostrils, and Enola could see that the message she had left using Hubcap Harry's satellite phone filled Allie's dark brown eyes: *Gvgeyui forever my beautiful daughter. I will love you in this lifetime and all others. I'm headed home.*

Muddy paw prints tattooed Enola's face, and in the sea of mud and debris, her left hand still clutched the crystal.

THE END

www.ingramcontent.com/pod-product-compliance
Lightning Source LLC
Chambersburg PA
CBHW061314170626
46817CB00001B/178